An Alpha's Choice

A Talon Pack Novel

CARRIE ANN RYAN

Author Highlights

Praise for Carrie Ann Ryan....

"Carrie Ann Ryan knows how to pull your heartstrings and make your pulse pound! Her wonderful Redwood Pack series will draw you in and keep you reading long into the night. I can't wait to see what comes next with the new generation, the Talons. Keep them coming, Carrie Ann!" –Lara Adrian, New York Times bestselling author of CRAVE THE NIGHT

"Carrie Ann Ryan never fails to draw readers in with passion, raw sensuality, and characters that pop off the page. Any book by Carrie Ann is an absolute treat." – New York Times Bestselling Author J. Kenner

"With snarky humor, sizzling love scenes, and brilliant, imaginative worldbuilding, The Dante's Circle series reads as if Carrie Ann Ryan peeked at my personal wish list!" – NYT Bestselling Author, Larissa Ione

"Carrie Ann Ryan writes sexy shifters in a world full of passionate happily-ever-afters." – *New York Times* Bestselling Author Vivian Arend

"Carrie Ann's books are sexy with characters you can't help but love from page one. They are heat and heart blended to perfection." *New York Times* Bestselling Author Jayne Rylon

Carrie Ann Ryan's books are wickedly funny and deliciously hot, with plenty of twists to keep you guessing. They'll keep you up all night!" USA Today Bestselling Author Cari Quinn

"Once again, Carrie Ann Ryan knocks the Dante's Circle series out of the park. The queen of hot, sexy, enthralling paranormal romance, Carrie Ann is an author not to miss!" *New York Times* bestselling Author Marie Harte

Praise for the Redwood Pack Series...

"You will not be disappointed in the Redwood Pack." *Books-n-Kisses*

"I was so completely immersed in this story that I felt what the characters felt. BLOWN AWAY." *Delphina's Book Reviews.*

"I love all the wolves in the Redwood Pack and eagerly anticipate all the brothers' stories." *The Book Vixen*

"Shifter romances are a dime a dozen, but good ones aren't as plentiful as one would think. This is one of the goods one." *Book Binge*

"With the hints of things to come for the Redwoods, I can't wait to read the next book!" *Scorching Book Reviews*

"Ryan outdid herself on this book." *The Romance Reviews*

Praise for the Dante's Circle Series...

"This author better write the next books quickly or I will Occupy Her Lawn until she releases more! Pure romance enjoyment here. Now go put this on your TBR pile—shoo!" *The Book Vixen*

"I, for one, will definitely be following the series to see what happens to the seven." *Cocktails & Books*

"The world of Dante's Circle series is enthralling and with each book gets deeper and deeper as does Carrie Ann's writing." Literal Addiction

Praise for the Montgomery Ink Series...

"Shea and Shep are so cute together and really offset each other in a brilliant way. " *Literal Addiction*
"This was a very quick and spicy read. I really enjoyed reading about Sassy, Rafe & Ian. I really hope there will be more of these three in the future." *Books n Kisses*

Praise for the Holiday, Montana Series...

"Charmed Spirits was a solid first book in this new series and I'm looking forward to seeing where it goes." *RR@H Novel Thoughts & Book Thoughts*
"If you're looking for a light book full of magic, love and hot little scenes on various objects, then this book is for you! You'll soon find that tables are no longer for eating meals of the food variety ... Bon appétit!" *Under the Covers*
"The book was well written and had the perfect setting the steamy bits where really really hot and the story one of sweet romance. Well done Carrie" *Bitten by Love Reviews*

DEDICATION

To those lost in the darkness.
There is a light, a break in the bleak.
Don't give up.

ACKNOWLEDGEMENTS

Five years ago when I wrote about Kade and Melanie in An Alpha's Path, the first novel of the Redwood Pack series, I never thought I would one day be writing a book about their grown son living in a world where the terrors he faces are even more dangerous than a demon with a plan of world domination. From the cover colors, the title, and to the idea that there is an answer through the darkness, Finn's story comes from his father's path. I knew that going in, only I didn't know I was on that same path as well.

I'll be honest and say Finn and Brynn's story broke me. These two took a toll on my heart and my brain, but in the end, after rewriting their complete story three times, An Alpha's Choice is ready for you.

I want to thank Kennedy Layne for holding my hand during my drafting stages. You have no idea how much you helped me by just listening. Thank you Chelle for taking me on during my panic and bringing their story to life with your edits. I adore you and now I *know* that we have a bright future together with our words. Thank you Rebecca and Dr Hubby for your help along the way. Finn and Brynn are brighter because of you. The Sprinting Ladies are always there for me, so thank you Shayla Black, Carly Phillips, Julie Kenner, Lexi Blake, Kennedy Layne, Angel Payne, and Jenna Jacob.

Also, thank you Steve Berry for listening to me talk while I tried to get through the plot issues I was having. Who knew a walk on the beach while we were searching for sharks, turtles, and sea glass would help spark the drive I needed to finish this book?

As always, thank you readers for being here with me every step of the way. For those of you just starting on this journey I hope you adore Finn and Brynn as much as I do. For those of you who have been here since the beginning—Finn is waiting...

An Alpha's Choice

Brynn Brentwood has spent the whole of her life protecting the Talon Pack through terrors only she will ever know. She's never asked for more in life other than to live to take her next breath and to ensure her family is safe. Regardless of her selfless wishes and the atrocities the former Alpha committed, she has always known that fate would provide for her as it had countless others. Fate is what has carried her through with one exception—upon meeting the one wolf who could be hers, he doesn't feel their bond.

Finn Jamenson has been broken more than once, left beaten and half dead—and that was before he was an adult and Heir of the Redwood Pack. When called upon to work with their allies, the Talons, he finds himself intrigued with a woman who his wolf doesn't claim as his own. Though he knows there could be something there, he refuses to tempt himself with a wolf who could never be his when his own mate could waiting for him.

The world changed in a blink of time and now the two wolves must fight as one—ignoring the burning temptation between them—when their people are threatened. With one wrong move, their homes could be destroyed and its up to Finn and Brynn to save them all...if only they could save themselves.

CHAPTER ONE

The echoes of helicopter blades chopping into the wind came closer with each passing breath. Brynn Brentwood fisted her hands at her sides, knowing there was nowhere to run, nowhere to hide.

They'd come for her family, her Pack. They'd come for her.

They'd come for answers no one truly wanted to hear, and yet, Brynn knew she'd fight to keep the truth at bay and keep what it revealed safe.

That was her job, her passion, her life.

The humans were coming for them, and the wolves at her back and at her side were as ready as they'd ever be. The reveal they'd always prepared for—and yet had prayed would never happen—was here.

The world would soon know that shifters were real...and close.

Brynn let out another breath, her eyes on the clearing around the wards of the den. When Leo, her now dead uncle, had shifted in front of a live-feed, he'd told the world—or whoever had been watching—that the things that went bump in the night were indeed real. Though her brother Gideon, the Alpha of

1

the Talon Pack, had killed Leo, the ramifications were far from over.

In fact, they were just beginning.

"Brynn, you hear that? They're coming."

Brynn looked over at her brother, Ryder, the Heir of the Pack and second eldest of them all. He'd fought by her side to defeat Uncle Leo, the elder named Shannon, the elder, and the handful of others who had tried to take over the Pack. He looked a little worse for wear with blood trickling down his side and dirt on his hands, but they all looked similar. They hadn't been able to shift and use their full strength to defeat the others. She and her family had been so afraid of showing what they truly were to outsiders, that they'd won the battle without shifting. As it turned out, all that work was for naught, though.

The humans—most likely soldiers—were coming. Were here. She could scent them on the wind, hear their feet pad along the forest floor. Oh, they might think they were being stealthy, but her wolf hearing could sense them.

Another thing the humans would fear about them.

Brynn thinned her lips and nodded at Ryder. "Gideon sent most of the Pack behind the wards and into the tunnels that connect to the Redwood Pack den. They'll be safe there. The humans can't see through the wards, nor can they even venture too close, but that won't stop them from doing all in their power to figure out how to stop us." They would find a way. Humans *always* found a way.

"You called your friends at the local precinct?" Brandon asked. He was the Omega of the Pack, the one who helped their emotional aches and pains. He was also her brother—one of the triplets. She couldn't hear fear in his voice, but there was the determination that came from being a Brentwood.

Brynn nodded. She knew a few people on the local police force, as well as another group of humans in the FBI and Homeland Security. It was her job in the Pack to blend in with the humans when she could, and form connections that might help them if the secret of their existence ever got out.

Only she prayed she'd never have to use those connections. There were wolves and humans who were on their side, strategically placed around the country to protect them if they were ever outed. Now they would have to use that web of protection and alliances and pray it did as intended.

"We can't just stay behind the wards and pray they'll go away," Gideon growled. "We need to go out there and show we won't lie down, but we also won't attack first."

Brynn agreed whole-heartedly. What they did this first day would set the tone for the rest of their lives. Or perhaps she'd wake up from this dream and everything would go back to the way it was.

The first human crawled up the rise, a tranquilizer gun in his hand and his buddies by his side.

No, this wasn't a dream. This was the real deal. Humans versus wolves.

"Come on," Gideon growled, taking his mate Brie with him. The fact that Brynn's big brother would even allow his mate to fight with him spoke of the importance of this first meeting.

Brynn stood between her brothers, her chin raised as they moved past the wards. Standing behind them and hiding was never an option. Those weaker than her were safe and hidden. Now it was her turn to show the humans the Pack wouldn't back down, nor would they attack without just cause.

"Don't kill anyone," Gideon said as he moved forward. "Only defend yourself. There's no hiding. Not anymore. But we can make this work. We *will* make this work."

She slid through the wards, the warm magic tingling across her skin. Witches and the Pack wolves had woven together the barrier to protect the Talons from the outside world. The strength of the wards relied on the strength of the Pack as a whole. Though her brother and the rest of her family had done their best to increase that strength, she knew they weren't as strong as the Redwoods. Betrayals and a past paved in blood had seen to that.

Brynn shook her head, exasperated with herself. She needed to get her head out of her ass and out of the past and onto the future. Or more accurately, the present. All they had to do was keep the humans from attacking them outright and keep things as calm as possible and maybe they'd have a chance at not ending up with a disaster in their hands.

When the first tranquilizer dart flew by her head as she passed through the wards, she knew the latter would only be a pipe dream.

Well, hell.

Gideon pulled Brie behind him and his mate let him. When the Alpha was in the mood he was in, it was best for Brie, a submissive wolf, to do as he said. Brynn knew one of the only reasons her sister-in-law was out here, was because Gideon needed to know she was safe, and the only way to do that was if she were near.

It felt like a blink of time later, and suddenly, Brynn had two humans flanking her, their guns raised, ready to pull the trigger. The others ducked and pushed at those who would take them in. Brynn did the same as she elbowed one man in the stomach, took his gun, dismantled it, then punched the other human in the face before he could shoot at her.

She didn't use her claws, didn't growl, didn't shift into her wolf form. She did all of this as the badass woman she was. Yet she knew it would never be enough. She'd fight, she'd scream, and she'd try to win, but unless their world found a balance as wolf and human, she'd never fully succeed.

No one would.

Another human soldier shot at her, and before she had a chance to duck out of the way, a human at her side tugged her closer. Her eyes widened, but he just frowned at her before nodding at some of his men.

That didn't make any sense. Why wouldn't he try to take her down as some of his team was? She frowned and looked closer at the humans attacking her family. It seemed only half of them truly shot at them while the others seemed to only want to get closer for some reason. She didn't understand *why,* but she knew it had to be important.

Someday.

She looked over at the man who had pulled her away, but he was gone, hidden among the trees surrounding the den.

What the hell?

"Stop what you're doing and hold up your hands!" a human called out. "We don't want to hurt you, but we will if we have to."

She tasted the lie on her tongue. Oh, this human wanted to hurt them and wouldn't feel a little bit bad about it. Was this what they had to look forward to? Was this the life they would lead for being different?

Her wolf pushed at her, and she tried to breathe. She didn't know what to do. This was so unlike her, so unlike every other decision she'd made. There was only one other decision in her life where she still had yet to find the right answer, but she wouldn't be thinking about him right now.

She couldn't afford to.

Ryder pulled at her waist and brought her closer, just as another human shot at them. She glared at her brother but nodded thanks just the same. She hated to be saved by any of them, but she could at least be grateful.

Standing here and getting shot at wasn't helping anyone. They couldn't just let themselves be taken in, but damn it, there had to be a way to talk to someone, make this...transition easier for everyone. It wasn't as if they were a complete secret from everyone, but this was getting ridiculous.

They weren't in a clearing, but rather a gathering of trees that kept some of them hidden. Brynn leaned into Ryder, her wolf aching to get out and fight for the protection of their den.

"They aren't going to listen to us," Ryder whispered. "The first people who showed up came with tranq guns that could actually work on us since those darts seem to be freaking huge. Not the best way to start."

Brynn frowned at the humans trying to surround her family. "They either knew we were already here and are using this as an excuse, or they just come in guns blazing at any threat."

"They aren't using actual guns, Brynn," Ryder said, his voice emotionless.

"I know," she whispered back. Something far more complicated than the fallout from a live feed of wolves changing into humans and back was going on here. "This was all an excuse to get us. Or something like it. They want us for some reason, and we don't know what branch of military or government this is. I don't like this, Ryder."

"None of us do, and Gideon holding us back is making it worse. Only I don't know how to make it better."

Brynn let out a breath then checked her phone. "None of my contacts are calling me back. What the hell is their use after all these years if they aren't going to help us."

"We don't know what's going on, Brynn. We don't know who Leo showed the feed to, and we don't know what others truly saw. The fact that those soldiers are here at all tells us it's nothing good, but we don't have the details."

And the details were where she and Ryder excelled. The rest of her brothers and cousins managed so many other intricacies of the Pack, but she and Ryder handled the details.

"Brynn Brentwood?" a voice called out over the distance. Her wolf stood on alert. Ryder let out a curse, but Brynn didn't feel the same.

"Finally," she muttered.

Gideon was at her side in a flash, his mouth in a snarl. "Who the fuck is that, and what do they want?"

Brynn wiped her hands on her pants and shook her head. "That is Alex Martinez. General Alex Martinez. And he's here to help us." She sucked in a breath. "At least I hope so. Trust me?"

Her brother and Alpha studied her face before nodding.

Her wolf whimpered at the show of respect, but Brynn pushed that away. She raised her chin and took one step forward, putting her body outside the coverage of the trees.

"General Martinez, it seems we have a lot to talk about."

The man who looked much older than Brynn but was over a century younger than her gave her a nod, his jaw tight. "It seems we do."

The world had changed with one breath; one slip of security, and now Brynn and the Talons would have to figure out the next step.

Or lose it all.

CHAPTER TWO

One Year Later

The bitter taste of burned coffee couldn't even be covered up by the heavy dose of sugar, caramel, and cream Brynn had added to her cup. Sometimes having an acute sense of taste really sucked.

She licked the remaining whipped cream off her lips and set down her cup; fully aware she wasn't drinking coffee in private. Nothing in her life was truly private. Not anymore.

Brynn smiled softly and brushed her long black hair from her shoulder, trying to look friendly, innocent, and as if she didn't have a care in the world. A total lie, but most people chose what they saw rather that what they should see.

The past year had just cemented that reasoning to her. When General Martinez had stepped foot near the Talon land, the game had changed yet again. The humans knew they existed. They knew shifters roamed around them; knew that some turned into so-called monsters. But they didn't know everything. It was Brynn's job to make sure they didn't know everything. Well, Brynn, the rest of her family, and the Redwoods.

Uncle Leo and his men had shifted into wolf form and back again on camera. *That* was what the public had seen. They'd seen the painful transition of bones breaking and tendons tearing. They saw humans shifted into wolves with claws and fangs. Then they'd seen Brynn and her family fight them in human form. They'd seen the show of strength, but they hadn't seen the death. The cameras had been destroyed by then. Thank the goddess. The humans had only seen a tiny part of who the shifters were. They hadn't seen a loving mated couple care for one another, hadn't seen a pup roll in the grass while chasing his tail.

They'd only seen the pain and fear that came with shifting. Brynn felt that same agony each time she turned wolf, but the bliss that wrapped around her soul when she connected with her shifter half was worth any pain.

Again, not that the humans knew that.

Since the Unveiling—yes, it had a name, thanks to the twenty-four hour media news cycle—her life had been on a rocky path, but she counted herself lucky she hadn't been strapped to a table to be studied...or killed outright for being different. It didn't matter that humans called themselves tolerant of all people. To most, Brynn and her family *weren't* people. In the hundred and fifty plus years of Brynn's life, she'd seen the worst of humanity as well as the worst of shifters, but she'd also seen the best. She'd seen the struggles that came with tolerance and acceptance of race, religion, sex, and creed. Life had taken great strides in finding an equality people could live with.

Only she wasn't human.

She'd never been human, not like some of her Pack and friends who had been turned later on in life.

She'd been born to wolf parents and raised as a pup. She'd had her first shift at age two, and had roamed the den and surrounding areas with two natures. She didn't know what life could be like without the constant struggle for control and the delicate balance that came with sharing a body with another spirit.

While some days she wished she were human so she could breathe in safety and not have to deal with Pack dynamics, fighting, and mates—she held back a wince at that last word—she knew she would never let anyone take away her wolf. Well, not like they could, but if there were somehow a magic potion where she could suddenly be fully human, she wouldn't take it.

Despite the fact that her family wasn't safe and her very life was on the line just being outside the den wards and in a public coffee shop, she wouldn't change who she was.

She was Brynn Brentwood, daughter of the former Alpha, sister of the current one. Dominant female of the Pack as her sister-in-law, Brie, was a submissive wolf. Brie held the title of Alpha female and ruled alongside her mate, Gideon. But no matter the strength Brie held and how she took care of internal matters in her own, gentler way, she would never be a dominant wolf. There was nothing wrong with that— no matter what some of the older wolves said. However, it made Brynn's life a little more hectic.

She ran a hand over her face. She couldn't afford to dwell on that right then. She had to keep alert, all the while looking as if she were happy and on her way to some of the boutiques to shop.

Yes. Coffee and shopping. *That* was how she was protecting her Pack at the moment.

The thing was, it didn't matter that it sounded ridiculous; she knew it would help in the long run. When General Martinez had taken control of the 'dispute' on Pack lands, he'd begun a new phase in the way of the shifter. Humans honestly had no idea what to do with them. Processing the concept of another species living amongst them, blending in with them, growing as one unit took time. They were at a standstill while people tried to come up with ideas regarding what to do about the 'shifter problem.'

Brynn rolled her eyes, knowing she probably looked like a lunatic. Probably not the best way to look calm and collected.

Washington currently had a few committees either being formed or already complete where they were trying to decide if shifters would lose their rights as Americans—if they were ever considered human, if they had a right to live on their own...if shifters needed to be studied or killed or even be forced to join a military group and fight to protect the country. Most shifters weren't out in the public as they hadn't been caught on camera like Brynn and her family had been. It was easier for them to hide what they were—safer, as well. But everyone knew that peace such as that couldn't last very long. Yes, some of those in Washington were actually shifters in hiding, but they had to be careful how they went forward. Deeply laid plans for the Unveiling only worked if people did their best not to create a war.

No one knew what to think, and that gave Brynn and her family time to create a better image than a snarling beast out of control. While Washington and the like tried to figure out what to do, Brynn and the others would show that they weren't evil, that they led normal lives.

That they shopped and drank coffee at little coffee houses and didn't bother a soul. And that was how Brynn found herself drinking her latte and waiting for a member of the Redwood Pack to join her. The

Redwoods were the Talons' allies and friends. They'd fought together in the Central war a couple of decades ago when a rogue Pack had called forth a demon to take over the world. And, of course, Brie had been a Redwood before she'd married Gideon, further strengthening their alliance.

Brynn closed her eyes, trying not to think of the way they could have cemented their alliance yet hadn't been able to. She swallowed hard, her hands fisting on her lap under the small round table. She lied to herself, saying it was only a way to bring the alliance closer.

Her heartbreak wasn't a thread to an alliance. It was a tactile piece of agony that pierced her body over and over again until the blessed numbness that came with defeat took over. She couldn't even rile up the anger in her veins anymore—so unlike her.

"What are you doing?"

That voice. That scent—the spicy blend of wolf and man.

Rage spiraled up within her, and she took a deep breath through her nose. It seemed she *could* get angry again. His presence broke through the numbness, the torture of knowing what she couldn't have, no matter what fate told her.

She forced herself to open her eyes and keep her emotions in check. She couldn't lash out in public—nor could she in private. If she let go, she'd break, and he'd see her weakness. He couldn't see her weak...couldn't see her at all.

He stood by her table, looming over her with the presence of an Heir to the Pack and the darkness of responsibilities layered on far too soon. He'd cut his hair since the last time she'd seen him. Usually, he liked to wear it long, brushing his shoulders like the Alpha of the Redwood Pack—and his father—Kade's

13

did. Now, it was still longer than most people wore, but he couldn't put it up in a stubby ponytail like he had before. He also hadn't shaved in a couple of weeks from what she could tell, so his strong jaw was covered in a dark beard that made her think of how it would feel on the sensitive skin of her inner thighs.

Shit. She couldn't think about that. He'd scent her arousal, and she'd be screwed—not literally in this case.

She focused instead on the jade green of his eyes that seemed to bore into her soul and burrow beneath the layer of ice she usually wore. Yet the damn man couldn't see what needed to be seen, needed to be felt.

How the hell was that even possible?

"Finn." Her voice was low, husky. Damn it.

He tilted his head, so like his wolf that she darted her eyes around the coffee shop, trying to see what the humans would do with two wolves in their midst. They might not know for sure if she were one, and they probably didn't know Finn was one, but from the way he stared at her with such intensity, she was afraid the others might see. He was too dominant, too close to his wolf. He couldn't hide it like the others, like she could, yet she wasn't sure he knew that.

Finn frowned at her then sat down across from her. "Why were you sitting like that when I came in? What's wrong?"

His voice was so low, so deep. She had to control herself and not let a shiver roll down her spine.

You. You're what's wrong. You're killing me with each breath; each word, and you don't even know it. You took my future, and yet you have no idea that you broke me at the same time. You know nothing, and there isn't a damn thing I can do about it because you can't see me as weak.

14

Yet she didn't say any of that. How could she? He didn't know why she felt empty inside. He didn't know why her wolf pressed up against her, begging her for touch, for a chance at something that would never be. Honestly, she had no idea what he knew, what he felt, only that he didn't feel the same as she did.

If he had, she'd have known.

"Nothing's wrong," she bit out. "Other than the fact you're late."

Finn's brows rose, but he didn't comment on the lie. Since he was such a strong wolf, he'd have been able to taste it on his tongue, but she didn't have the desire to deal with anything like that right then. All she wanted to do was get this day over with and get home. Once she was behind the wards, behind her own door, she'd shake and break and find a way to keep going. It wasn't the end of the world, she told herself. She wouldn't let it be.

"If you say so. And I'm not that late. I hit traffic on the way over here. This place is closer to your d— home than mine." She snorted at his near-mistake at the use of the word den. They didn't want to advertise their species at the moment, but he'd caught himself in time.

"You should have left earlier, then," she snapped quietly. She sucked in a breath, aware her wolf was far too close to the surface. She needed to regain some semblance of control so she could get on with their day. Lashing out at him, or worse, letting her eyes glow gold and wolf-like wouldn't help matters. "Sorry, the coffee tastes horrible, and, apparently, it's making me act bitchy."

"An apology? How unlike you," he said smoothly. He stood then and held his hand out. "Let's get shopping, then. Throw out your cup and we'll find you another place."

She stood without taking his hand, her chin raised. "I'm not one of your little groupies, Finn. I don't need your help." She tossed the cup and took another deep breath, aware others were watching. Of course, from the outside, it looked like a bitter woman fighting with a man, but still, she needed to keep her emotions in check. That would be easier said than done.

Finn let out a sigh. "Let's go, Brynn. I'll get you something shiny."

She just narrowed her eyes but kept a smile on her face. She couldn't scare the little humans. "Shiny is good," she said, trying to rein her wolf in.

Finn smiled back, but it didn't reach his eyes. He knew something was off, but he'd never know the truth.

It wasn't like she could tell him, after all.

The man at her side, who irritated her to no end, was the one man in all the world fate had decreed to be hers. He was her mate, her other half, her peace.

Yet he didn't feel the same pull, didn't acknowledge that she was *his* other half.

Finn was her mate, yet she wasn't his.

Fate royally sucked.

CHAPTER THREE

Finn Jamenson did not understand women. Oh, he might have tons of them in his family, and had had his fair share in his bed, but for the life of him, he couldn't understand them. One minute they were smiling, the next they were snapping at him, ready to tear his throat out for daring to be late.

Okay, so maybe he shouldn't have been late meeting Brynn at the coffee place before they'd gone shopping earlier, but he'd spent twenty minutes in his car outside trying to calm himself down. And for once, it wasn't him trying to calm his wolf down. Instead, his wolf did nothing while Finn tried to figure out how the hell he was going to handle this situation. The man wanted the woman inside that building. He wanted to cup her face, taste her lips, and kiss her until both of them were gasping for breath.

He wanted to slam her against the nearest wall and slide his hand down the front of her jeans so he could feel how wet she was. Because damn it, he *knew* she'd be wet. He could scent her arousal every time she was near him, and it wasn't like it was one-sided either. His damn cock had zipper marks along the side of it since he was hard all the freaking time around her.

Yet neither of them had done anything about it. He figured it was because she just didn't like him. He wasn't sure what he'd done to deserve her ire, but he *was* only in his thirties while she was over a hundred fifty. Maybe she just didn't like younger pups who were more dominant than her. That made sense, considering she and her wolf held the strength that most dominants would never attain. Only a few wolves were stronger than her, he figured, and he was one of them. He couldn't help it; he'd been born this way. Add in the fact that he held the mantle and bonds of being the Heir to a rival Pack since before he'd started kindergarten, and his wolf held more power than most thought he could deal with.

Hell, most days he wasn't sure he could handle it either.

He'd never made a move on Brynn, and she'd yet to make a move on him either. Despite the fact that both of them clearly wanted each other, he didn't think they'd ever scratch that itch. She wasn't his mate. His wolf would have felt the pull, or at least pushed him closer if that had been the case. Instead, his wolf had been oddly silent.

Maybe *oddly* wasn't the best word for that. His wolf was usually silent. It took a lot of energy to keep in control, but his wolf didn't push him daily on things like going for a run or needing to fight a battle. It was more of a subtle burn that ached inside him at all times. He didn't have the normal pushes like others said they felt.

He figured it was because he wasn't a normal wolf. Not anymore. Not since the demon Caym had almost killed him as a child. The memory of broken bones and a scream that would never come filled his mind and he held himself unnaturally still, afraid if he were to move, he'd break again. He could still scent the blood of his uncle Josh, who had almost died as well, his throat slit, his eyes wide as he'd reached for Finn.

Finn let out a breath. He didn't need to think about that day, that pain. In fact, he needed to get his mind off demons and Brynn altogether.

He and Brynn would never get in bed and act out their baser urges because they weren't mates. And while he could sleep with other wolves, witches, and humans, knowing he would never mate with them, he wasn't sure he could do that with Brynn. For one thing, it would probably fuck up the delicate alliance he had with her, not to mention the one between their two Packs.

Plus, he had a feeling that once he had Brynn, he wouldn't be able to stop at just one taste.

And that would be bad for both of them when they met their *real* mates.

So Finn would do his best to stay away from her and the temptation that came with being in her presence. He could do that. Maybe.

It would be best for both of them if they could give each other space to get over this attraction of theirs. Fucking just to satisfy an urge, where in the end he'd wind up in pieces wouldn't solve anything. He couldn't stand the thought of wanting Brynn as a man, only to find out later that he'd lost a chance at true happiness with his mate because he'd been confused and focusing on impulses he shouldn't have.

And that right there was why he had to take a step back. He sounded like such an asshole. He wasn't usually like this—he was usually the one who joked and tried to alleviate pressure. Instead, he could only think of Brynn and his personal issues, rather than the issues at hand.

For instance, the reason why he was currently in his parents' home waiting for the rest of his family to show up so they could begin their meeting. Most of the family hadn't shown up yet, and his parents were upstairs getting dressed after...well, Finn didn't want to think about that either. He held back a grin. At least he knew Kade and Melanie Jamenson still couldn't keep their hands off each other after all these years.

Once everyone arrived, they were supposed to discuss the next phase of action with regards to their safety and the full Unveiling. Instead, all he could think about was how much his dick hurt.

Thankfully he wasn't fully hard right then since Brynn wasn't in the room, but in a den full of wolves with an acute sense of smell, being turned on at the thought of another wolf was embarrassing. Hell, it had made puberty a fucking nightmare.

"What is with that face?" his cousin Charlotte asked. She frowned at him as she pulled her long, black, curly hair into a ponytail. She was forever fidgeting with her hair, either covering her face as much as possible or making sure it didn't touch the back of her neck. He understood her ticks, but he wished there was a way he could help fix the reasoning behind them.

"What do you mean?" he asked, pushing thoughts of his worries for Charlotte and his need for Brynn from his brain.

The Talon wolf wasn't his mate. End of story.

Charlotte gave him a side-eye and he snorted. "You look conflicted and yet angry at the same time. So what's up?"

He shook his head. "Just going through things. No worries."

She stared at him.

"Really. I swear. I know your dad was the Omega, but I don't need to tell you everything I'm feeling. If it were a huge deal, I'd tell you. Okay?"

She rolled her eyes, letting his wolf relax since he hadn't hurt her with his careless words. "I worry about you because you're my family, friend, and roommate. Not because of who my dad is. You know better than that, Finn Jamenson."

He shrugged, though he knew he had probably been an ass just then, too. Apparently, it was a common theme these days. "Thanks for worrying," he said, meaning it. He worried about her, too. That's what made them friends, cousins, and Packmates. "Though at some point, don't you think we should get our own places?"

Charlotte blinked at him. They'd only been living together for the past year. Before that, he'd lived with his other cousin, Brie. There was enough space that he could have lived alone like some of his brothers and most of his cousins, but he liked the company. He had a dozen male cousins and siblings he could have lived with, but Brie and Charlotte were the ones that could deal with him and his wolf the best. They didn't crowd him or challenge his wolf. In fact, Brie had been so submissive, she'd helped settle his wolf in a way he missed. He'd been able to help her wolf out too since that's the way their wolves worked. Charlotte wasn't submissive, but she had a caring way about her that soothed, as well. The darkness within her matched his own, albeit on a different and hidden level.

"I like staying with you," she said softly. "I don't like being alone. And while I love Mom and Dad, I'm a little too old to keep living with them."

Finn reached out and played with her ankle, knowing she needed touch but space, as well. She'd been through hell growing up before Maddox and Ellie had found her chained to a wall and had taken her in as their own. The fact she was actually Ellie's sister and not her daughter wasn't something they discussed. Their twisted family tree made for a confusing bedtime story. Charlotte was family and that was that.

"I like having you around, too," he said softly.

"I love the two of you so much."

Turning at the sound of Brie's voice, Finn was on his feet in a flash and had her in his arms just as quickly. She wrapped her arms around his waist and sighed into him. "Missed you, Brie," he growled softly, inhaling her scent. She calmed him with just her presence. She was family, even if she didn't live in their den anymore. "Love you, too," he whispered. "Since you've married that oaf over in the Talons, I hardly ever see you anymore."

Charlotte laughed behind him and tugged Brie away so she could hug her, too. "Finn's an idiot, but I love and miss you more."

Brie stepped back once Charlotte released her and smiled at both of them. Despite the fact he called Gideon an oaf, he knew the Alpha was the best thing for Brie. He'd never seen her so happy, so cared for, so strong.

The world might have been crashing down around them in the past year, and their lives were at risk just for being wolves, but he knew Brie was in her element with her mate. She'd taken to the role of being the Alpha's mate better than anyone could have hoped for. He'd been so fucking worried when she'd first told him of her potential bond with Gideon. The two of them had taken the rocky road to finding their way through their relationship, but Finn had a feeling both were better for it.

Finn frowned. "Wait. Why are you here? Not that I don't love you being here, but I'm confused."

Brie gave him a sad smile. "A few of the Talons are coming to meet. We took the tunnels rather than driving over since we're under such surveillance outside the wards."

The tunnels had taken almost fifteen years to complete, but they connected the two Packs over the miles that separated them. Not only did they have to deal with the natural boundaries, but they also had to add in the wards and magical influences to keep their dens safe from outsiders. It was one way they were able to protect their dens from those that would attack them for the blood that ran through their veins.

Finn cursed. He hated that he felt like he lived in a prison. What had once been a place of safety from the outside world, now felt like the bars of captivity. They could come and go as they wanted, but the humans watched them. Or, at least, they watched the Talons since that's where it had all started. In the past year, humans had started following around enough Talons that they'd found the Redwood den. Either that, or they'd known all along. He wasn't sure exactly *what* the government knew at this point. Just one more reason they were meeting. They couldn't sit back anymore and wait to see what the humans would do.

The full extent of what Brie had said hit him and he froze fractionally before forcing himself not to look like he was on edge. "Who came with you?" His voice was lower than usual, and he caught the curious look in Brie's and Charlotte's gazes, but he ignored them.

"Gideon, Ryder, and Brynn," she said slowly, her eyes narrowing. "The rest are at the den, holding the fort so to speak. Gideon thought it would be best not to bring the whole crew on Redwood Pack land. The four of us, plus two soldiers is enough."

It made sense, even though he couldn't quite think. As Alpha, Gideon would need to talk with Kade about what their plans were. Though they met in neutral territory as often as possible, sometimes it was necessary to meet in one of the dens, showing their trust in the pact. They also had almost daily online meetings, but everyone was careful about what they said, as no matter how good they were with technology, they could never be sure they were completely safe. Not anymore.

Ryder, as the Heir of the Talon Pack, did much of the same things as Finn did. The two of them helped their Alpha keep their Pack safe, as well as carry the burden of being connected to so many wolves at once. The Alphas held the most, but without the Heir, it would be too much. One day, Kade would step down and Finn would be Alpha. Finn just prayed that it wouldn't happen as it had before. When Finn's grandfather Edward had died protecting them all, Kade had become Alpha on a battlefield covered in blood, and Finn had gained the responsibility of a Pack as a toddler.

Ryder, though a good Heir from what Finn could see, wouldn't always remain an Heir. When Gideon and Brie had a child, the firstborn son would become the Heir when he was old enough, unless something tragic happened like it had in Finn's case. Actually, with the way the moon goddess had changed the dynamics ever so slightly with his family, their firstborn son *or* daughter could be the Heir.

When Finn had been forced to carry the bonds of Heir, he'd altered the timeline of when the next round of power would be exchanged. His siblings were all becoming the next in the hierarchy far too young. He knew it wasn't his fault, but he couldn't help but blame himself. But with the changing of the guard, the

Redwoods were in a special position where they had a former set of power holders who were in the same shape and at the same endurance level as the current ones. It only made them stronger.

It was different for the Talons, he knew. They'd had the change of the guard through pain and blood because Gideon and Brynn's father had been a tyrant rather than an Alpha. Finn didn't know everything, but he knew it had been bad. Maybe one day Brynn would tell him the extent of what had happened so he'd be able to help.

He almost froze again.

No, he wouldn't be talking to Brynn about that. She wasn't his mate. She wasn't even his friend. She couldn't be, not with the attraction they held for each other and the lack of ability to do anything about it.

Finn cleared his throat, aware the girls had started talking about something else when he'd been lost in his own thoughts. It wasn't unlike him to do that when he was in the company of those he trusted, not when his mind went to the darkness of his past more than it should, but he didn't like it. He wanted to live in the present, only he couldn't cut those ties.

"Good, you guys are here," Kade, Finn's father, and Alpha of the Redwood Pack said as he made his way into the room. He strolled toward them, his hair still messy from whatever he'd been doing upstairs with Melanie. The strain around his eyes wasn't easy to see, but Finn had spent his whole life studying his father to ensure one day he'd become the Alpha he needed to be. The past year had been hell on all of them, but the Alphas had borne the worst strain. They had to balance the line of politics and war, and yet ensure their Pack *felt* safe within the den wards. It wasn't an easy task, and as time moved forward, Finn wasn't sure the task would be possible.

"Uncle Kade," Brie said with a smile. Kade opened his arms, and Brie stepped right into them. Some of the tension in the Alpha's shoulders eased, and Finn held back a smile. Sometimes, Finn wasn't sure Brie was aware of what she could do with her submissive nature, but right then, he had a feeling his cousin knew *exactly* what she was doing. After all, she was married to an Alpha.

Kade pulled away and ran a hand through his hair. "We're not bringing in everyone today, just a few of us since Gideon agreed not to bring his whole Pack onto our land. That means it's pretty much the few of us in this room. We'll let the others know what we come up with, and frankly, won't make any new decisions without them, but we still need to talk."

Charlotte frowned. "Then why am I here? I mean, not that I mind being included, but I don't hold a title in the Pack. I'm just me."

Finn snorted. "There's nothing *just* about you."

She grinned at him, a rare true smile.

Kade snorted. "You're here because you're part of our future generation, and you're best friends with Finn. He might need you after the talk we have today."

At that cryptic statement, his father left the room, presumably to go to the meeting area where Gideon would show up. Finn stood there, his eyes wide. "Why would I need you, Charlotte? What the hell is going on?"

He looked toward Brie, who winced. "What, Brie?"

"I don't know everything, but you *know* this isn't the first meeting we've had, right? There are plans being set it motion, and whatever happens today, know that I love you and will support you no matter what."

A sense of foreboding slid over his skin. "Brie."

She shook her head. "I can't. Come on to the back. The others will be in the room by now. I wanted to come through before the actual meeting because I miss you guys and I'd rather be here as family first before I'm the Alpha's mate."

She took Charlotte's hand and made her way to the back of the house, leaving Finn there, speechless. The strength she held constantly surprised him, though he knew it shouldn't. It would take the strength of a thousand dominant wolves for a submissive wolf to handle and mate with an Alpha. Brie had that reserve of strength in spades.

Finn took a deep breath and moved toward where the others were gathering. His mind tried to follow the path where his father would lead him, but he couldn't think clearly. Not when the exotic and floral scent that was the woman he couldn't have filled his nostrils, sending the human half of him into straight lust. Jesus, he couldn't think with her around, couldn't breathe. It wasn't a mating bond—that much he knew—but that damned itch wouldn't leave him the fuck alone.

He rolled his shoulders, begged his cock to keep down, and walked through the door to the meeting room.

There she was.

All dark hair and bright blue eyes. Her strong cheekbones stood out, her jaw set as she met his gaze. Hell, she *hated* him, and he didn't know why. He hadn't done a thing to hurt her, and yet it looked like she wanted to snap his spine.

Or rather, snap his spine *after* fucking him hard against the wall.

That was yet another reason he couldn't get a bead on the woman in front of him.

"Finn." Ryder nodded at him, and Finn gave him a chin tilt back.

"Ryder."

"You're here," Gideon growled then looked down at Brie, who had apparently elbowed him in the gut. "Good to see you, Finn."

Finn held back a smile at the way the big Alpha softened at the touch of his mate. Finn wanted that, *craved* that. He'd seen the way his family had fallen, one by one, with their mates. Seen the way they raised their children and fell more in love each and every day. He couldn't wait to have that with someone.

If only he could get *her* out of his mind so he could get on with it.

"Let's get started," Kade said softly. "Most of us already know why we're here."

Finn frowned. He didn't like being left out of the loop, and he had a feeling he wasn't going to like where this was going.

"Since the humans found out about us, we've done our best to keep calm, keep rational," Kade continued. "Only a few of us have been outed, and the government doesn't know what to do with us because we've had the right people in power all this time. But things are coming, we know this. Those who want to hurt us, who want to *control* us, are getting louder."

"We have fires burning within the circles that will gain traction in the government and sects we've been following all this time," Gideon growled. The Alpha spoke in a growl at all times it seemed. "But there is one thing we need to keep going. The human's perception of us."

Finn tilted his head, confused. What did this have to do with him?

"You're talking propaganda." Brynn's voice slid over him, even as the barbs in her words did, as well.

"We're talking perception," Kade said. "My nephew Parker is out in the world, talking to other Packs and doing his best to connect all of us so we're ready. Not every Pack is ready to align themselves with others. There are centuries-long tensions, and even more fear when it comes to wanting to hide from what the humans could do to us if they tried. But while he is doing that, we need to make sure the humans do not fear us."

"But shouldn't they?" Charlotte asked, her voice soft. "Shouldn't they fear us, just a little?"

Kade let out a sigh. "Yes, and no. But right now, they know nothing about what we *are*. And what humans do not understand, they want to destroy. We aren't the first people to have this happen."

"You're saying you want to put a face on us," Finn said slowly. "You want the humans to see us as one of them, even if we're not."

Finn's mother, Melanie, nodded. "Yes, hon. We want them to see us interacting with the world and not killing them outright. Because, hell, we *aren't* killers. They need to know that."

"And what happens when that lack of fear turns on us?" Brynn asked.

Gideon raised his chin. "Then we take the next step. We *will* protect our people. But first, we need humans to see us as *real*. Not monsters."

"What does this have to do with the people you asked to be here?" Finn asked.

Kade let out a breath. "We need a person from each Pack to act as a representative within the world. We already have a few of us out there trying to mingle and acting like nothing is wrong. But now we need those people to do it daily, to interact and not shy away if a camera takes a photo of you smiling." He turned toward Finn. "I need you and Brynn to continue doing as you've been doing, but make it stronger. Show the world that we aren't monsters. Prove to them we can live within their world and within our own. You and Brynn have laid the groundwork in the past year. Now, make it *more*."

Finn cursed inwardly. It all sounded like a fine plan if it had been *anyone* else. But having to be near Brynn day in and day out until they figured out a way to keep their people safe? He wasn't sure if he would be able to do that. He met Brynn's gaze, the anger in them almost tactile.

He wasn't sure she would be able to do that either.

Because the more they were around each other, the hotter the flames burned. And one day, they wouldn't be able to tame the fire. When that day came, he wasn't sure who would make it out in one piece.

If either of them could.

CHAPTER FOUR

B rynn slammed her fist into the wall, the drywall giving in, creating a hole where a slab once stood. The pain sliced down her arm, a dull throb instead of something more serious thanks to the blood in her veins. Her body shook, and she tried her best not to scream.

She'd held the fire, the rage, inside throughout the entire meeting with the Redwoods and had even made it to her home before she'd broken. She was lucky she'd lasted that long.

How could her brother, her Alpha, do this to her? Didn't he see the pain on her face, feel the agony in the bond she held with him as Alpha? Her other brother Brandon, the Omega, who could feel all of the emotions of the Pack, would probably be able to feel her anguish, but damn it, why couldn't her Alpha of a brother? Why did he have to put her through the pain of being with the one man who hated her? Hated her enough to ignore the bond they could have with one another—if he could even feel it at all.

It made no sense.

She'd been too good at hiding her feelings, she knew that. But she'd always done that. When her father had almost killed her, she'd done her best not to cry. Because if she cried, it would have only made him happier and hurt her brothers and cousins at the same time. So she'd held it all in, even when she was dying inside. And now she was doing it all again because she didn't want the others to know the one man who could have been hers didn't feel the same way.

She'd been alive long enough to think she might never find a mate, and when she finally had, he didn't reciprocate, didn't show her a damn thing. Son of a bitch. She hated that she let Finn do this to her. So what if he was the sexiest man she'd ever met? So what if he held enough dominance that he'd be able to take her in bed? He'd be able to fuck her hard into the mattress and not wince when her claws dug into his back. He'd ride her like a fucking cowboy and keep her sated.

She gritted her teeth. It wasn't as if she *needed* a man to fuck her hard. She could give herself an orgasm just fine. In fact, that's *all* she'd been doing for way too fucking long.

The sexual tension riding her probably wasn't helping the situation with the Redwoods and humans, but damn it, it was all Finn's fault. Everything was Finn's fault.

And now she sounded like a whiny little teenager instead of an adult woman with enough strength to kill a man with one hand.

Damn it.

She pulled her hand out of the wall and flexed her fingers. Thankfully, she didn't think anything was broken. She was *not* in the mood to deal with Walker, the Pack's Healer and another of her brothers, if she'd fucked her hand up. He'd have questions, and the man had a way of getting answers out of her even when she'd rather remain silent. He saw right through her. Hell, *all* her brothers and cousins did. Mitchell and Max may not be her brothers, but they'd been raised in the same fire and brimstone she had. They'd been by her side during the internal wars and struggles that had led them to where they were today.

She flexed her hand once more and closed her eyes, knowing she needed to keep her mind out of the past and even off the bleak future. It might kill her with each step, each breath, to be by Finn's side and not be able to do a single thing about her need for him, but she'd get over it. She had to. There was no other choice.

A soft knock on the door broke through her pity party and she inhaled, holding back a curse at the owner of the scent.

Of course, it would be Brie at her door. It wouldn't be anyone else. It *had* to be the cousin and one of the best friends of the man on her mind. Brie was her Alpha's mate, *her* Alpha female. And a freaking submissive wolf, who saw far too much with those eyes of hers.

Brynn took a deep breath and made her way to the door, opening it as she tried to keep her face neutral. Showing her internal struggle wouldn't help anyone. She couldn't let Brie know what was going on inside her head, couldn't let the world know. Because if she did, then it would be real. Then Finn would know he'd hurt her just by not acknowledging her.

He didn't have the right to know he'd hurt her.

A snarl slipped through her lips and Brie's eyes widened.

Way to go with the whole looking neutral and natural thing.

"Is everything okay?" Brie asked. The other woman shook her head. "Of course, it's not okay. I'm here because I *know* something's off with you, Brynn. Gideon told me to leave it alone, but he doesn't know me well at all if he thinks I'm just going to sit back when I know something is wrong." Brie crossed her arms over her chest and tilted her head. "Now, are you going to invite me in so we can talk about it? Or are you going to let me ramble on out here on your porch where anyone can come up and hear what I'm saying?"

Brynn couldn't help it. She laughed. "I swear, sometimes you're like a puppy, not a wolf."

Brie flashed a smile that turned into a slight snarl. "Don't mess with me, Brynn. I might be little, but I bite. Hard. Just ask Gideon."

Brynn stood back, her body shaking. "Please don't talk about biting my brother like that again. I'm going to have nightmares now, thinking of him and you doing...things." She shuddered again. "Nope. Not going there. It's bad enough I have to watch him watch you like you're a baby lamb going off to slaughter."

Brie snorted and sat on Brynn's couch. "I don't think he looks at me like I'm a baby lamb. More like a piece of candy he can't wait to unwrap and suck on."

Brynn held out her hands. "No. For the love of the goddess. Please stop."

"You started it."

"And you finished it well enough so we never have to talk about biting, sucking, or unwrapping again." Despite herself, Brynn laughed. Brie had a way about her that settled Brynn's wolf just by being near her. It was mostly because Brie was submissive, but Brynn had a feeling it would be the case even if Brie were a dominant wolf.

Brynn sank onto the couch next to Brie, knowing that she had to keep her emotions in check. Being too emotional wouldn't do any good. So what if she was dying inside? She had a job to do. A job that included working side by side with the one wolf who could hurt her just by breathing.

Easy.

"Are you going to tell me what's wrong?" Brie asked, their moment of levity over.

"I'm fine," she lied.

Brie raised a brow. "I so don't believe you. You've been out of sorts for a year now, and today was even worse."

"You've only known me for a year, Brie." Gideon mating with Brie had brought Finn into her life. She may have seen him in the distance in the past thirty years the Redwoods and Talons had been working together, but she hadn't truly *met* him until Gideon and Brie's mating ceremony. Finn had only been a child when she and her family had stepped in after years of war to try and help defeat the Centrals. She hadn't seen him then, and since the moon goddess wasn't truly evil, she wouldn't have known Finn was her mate at that time anyway. They might have been fated to be together, but maturity mattered. Fifteen years later, when her friend Quinn had mated Finn's sister Gina—the first mating of a Talon in far too long, and the first mating between the Packs—she'd only seen Finn from afar. He'd been an adult at that point, but still far too young for her.

Then he'd come to the den with Brie, and she'd been lost.

He'd looked right through her.

No, that was a lie. He'd checked her out, his wolf glowing in his eyes as if he liked what he saw. But that had been it. He'd been a male reacting to a female he wanted to fuck.

He hadn't been a man falling to his knees in rapture at the idea of a mate.

She'd been so *angry* when he hadn't blinked, hadn't felt what she'd felt. She might not have spoken about it to his face, but there would have been some form of recognition. She'd seen the reactions of others finding their mates enough to know what Finn should have done if they'd been mates and he'd felt it.

Of course, in the worst-case scenario, he *could* feel the potential of a bond and he *chose* to ignore it. She didn't want to think about that. Because if that were the case, he'd seen her—*felt* her—and rejected her. It hurt to think that she'd rather fate have fucked up and given her a mate that couldn't feel what she did rather than one who didn't want her at all.

Her wolf whimpered, a sign of weakness she'd rather chew her own foot off than show, and she ground her teeth.

Brie sat next to her, studying her face intently. "You're in pain, Brynn. I can feel it, and you damn well know Brandon can. Gideon can as well, but he has so much on his plate, he's choosing not to be the overprotective brother and try to fix all your problems for you. At least that's how he's choosing to deal with this for now. I don't know how much our Alpha can hold back when it comes to you. He'd tear up the world more than it already is to protect you."

Tears filled Brynn's eyes and she cursed. She cleared her throat. "I think you're confusing the two of us. He'd start *another* war for you."

Brie let out a sigh. "You're his baby sister. It doesn't matter you're over a century old. He'd do anything for you. He'd do anything for any of his brothers and cousins, too. That's the kind of man he is and what makes him a wonderful yet sometimes overbearing Alpha."

She snorted, knowing the overbearing part was accurate. "I'm fine." She let out a breath. "I'm going to be fine. How's that?" Because she wouldn't let this all-consuming agony take over her life and risk her Pack. They were worth more than a bleeding wolf with no mate. Far more.

"I wish you'd tell me what's wrong, Brynn. You're my sister now. You know I'd do anything for you."

"I've never had a sister, you know."

Brie grinned. "Growing up with all those boys must have been hell. I don't know how you and my Aunt Cailin did it. At least I have girls in my generation."

"I didn't mind it, actually." She frowned. "They were there for me in the darkest days. Even when they were overbearing and so *male*, they were my blood. You know?"

Brie sighed, sadness filling her eyes. "I do. Gideon told me some of what your father did to all of you, but not everything."

Brynn stiffened. No. She wouldn't think about that, wouldn't think about the past. Wasn't it just a few minutes ago she'd told herself she'd live in the present? And yet, here she was, thinking about the piercing screams and endless trails of blood and memories. She'd learned long ago not to scream, even when it hurt too much to bear.

Brie held out her hands, careful not to touch Brynn. Oh so careful. "He didn't tell me your secrets. You know your brother would never do that." There was an edge to Brie's words, and Brynn relaxed marginally. The woman defended her mate at the same time she tried to soothe Brynn. There was a strength there that others hadn't bothered to see.

Brynn let out a breath. "I do. I'm sorry." She ran a hand over her face. "I'm just a little off. It'll pass."

"If you're sure." It didn't sound like Brie believed her one bit, but there wasn't anything she could do about that at the moment. "I actually came over here to see what your plans were with Finn before we head back over to the house to meet with the rest of the family. I figured you might want to talk it over with just me before you're bombarded by the testosterone that is the Brentwood men."

Brynn held back a smile at the thought of the male-dominated family she lived in, even if she winced at just the mention of Finn's name. Fuck, this wasn't going to be easy.

"Finn and I didn't talk much about what our plans were, other than meeting for coffee. Again." She tried to forget the way he'd made her feel when he'd prowled toward her in the shop, the way her wolf went on alert, begging for scraps of affection that would never come.

Fuck this. She wasn't some damsel in need of saving. If he didn't want her, then fuck it all. She didn't like who she was becoming at the mere thought of him. She pushed thoughts of loss and bonds away once again, locking the key on the vault of Finn.

Fuck.

Him.

"I know the two of you have done the whole be-nice-in-public thing a few times over the past year, and that's why you were chosen. But I don't know if coffee will do it."

"I know. We've shopped before. Or rather, I've pretended to shop and he's growled behind me, apparently bored out of his mind."

Brie grinned. "It's because Charlotte and I used to force him to go with us when things were...safer."

Safer. Because now most in the Pack never left the den. It wasn't safe. The military and government might still be in transition, and they weren't a hundred percent clear on how they would react in the near future, but that didn't mean things were easy. The everyday humans were a fear. As wolves, they couldn't fight back like they should in case a human *did* provoke them. They couldn't spill blood and protect themselves. They had to be careful. Everything stood on an edge so thin, Brynn wasn't sure where it began and the end tapered off.

If they weren't careful, the humans would fear them more than they already did, and things would go downhill fast for the wolves and her family.

"For now, Finn and I will continue to do what we normally do...just do it more often. We're planning on meeting tomorrow, and I know we will probably go out each day. We'll look...normal." As normal as she could be by his side but that was neither here nor there.

Brie nodded. "I know we're putting a lot on your shoulders, and you won't be the only ones that go out. Eventually, we'll put a few more out. Not too many at once so we don't make the humans feel as though we're taking over."

Brynn snorted. "I wish we could just have it out and throw up our hands. Just tell them that we're here, we've *always* been here, and we're not going anywhere. But instead, we have to be careful because the world isn't like it once was. One wrong move and everything can fall down around us."

"I hate it, too. I hate that we can't be ourselves and that we're always scared. I mean, my parents met *outside* the den. They were outside in public and were normal. My mom was human and became a wolf because the Centrals forced it on her, but she would

39

have chosen to become one of us on her own like my Aunt Melanie did. Now it's almost as if we're forced into our own cages because we aren't sure who knows which of us can shift."

Brynn let out a breath. "Thank the goddess they can't tell from blood tests."

Brie nodded. That little detail had to be due to the moon goddess because Brynn had been sure medical tests would have revealed who they were. Instead, their blood came up as human. That meant that if the government ever tried for mandatory testing by blood, they would come up empty. There were other ways to find out their true nature, but at least they were safe from that.

For now.

Science was always evolving.

"Just integrate yourself and look harmless," Brie said with a strained grin.

"Sure. Because your cousin can look harmless, considering he's the size of a truck."

"He can grin and look like he's your best friend. You're the one I'm more afraid of, honestly."

Brynn sat up straight. "What do you mean? He's more dominant that I am?"

Brie shook her head. "Yeah, but you're not that far behind. He might have shadows in his eyes because of what happened to him as a kid, but he does his best to look carefree. You always look like you're ready to kick ass and take names."

"I've had to be that way," she grit out.

Brie held up her hands. "I know. Believe me, I know. Your family grew up differently than mine, and it shaped how we interact with the world today. Plus, you're a dominant woman without a title in the Pack because the moon goddess was on crack when she handed out roles. You're constantly fighting dominance challenges because others don't know where to place you. It's on them, I know, but because of that, you always look like you're ready to protect what's yours."

Brynn's shoulders fell. "It's not my fault others don't know how to handle me. I'm not a bitch."

"And I didn't say you were. I said you're ready to protect. How is that me calling you a bitch? You saved my life, Brynn. You've saved countless lives and never asked for a thank you. The only thing you've done is show me how to be the Alpha female of a Pack, and yet not be the most dominant."

The two of them were in a weird balance. In any other Pack, Brie would have been the most dominant wolf in the Pack. She'd not only mated Gideon and would have inherited some of his strength in doing so, but the moon goddess matched wolves with a purpose. Because Brie was submissive, things were a little trickier. She held the power of the Alpha and ruled with a swift grace Brynn had never seen the likes of, but she wasn't dominant. She would never be dominant, and that was fine for Brie and most of the Pack.

Others would just have to get over it. Because while Brie might not want to fight, she *could,* and was freaking amazing at it. Brynn was there as backup because damn it, she was fucking strong, too.

"The dominance challenges are getting on my last nerve," Brynn admitted. Many things were getting on her last nerve it seemed. The Pack, Finn, this assignment...

"Is Katherine still being a bitch?" Brie asked, her face scrunched.

Katherine was the lead dominant female that kept trying to take Brynn's place. She'd been on Iona's side when Iona had tried for Brie back when Gideon and

Brie had first mated. Iona had backed down and had even almost died protecting Brie when a betrayal had almost ended her life. Katherine, on the other hand, had stepped into Iona's place and wanted to push Brynn around.

Nothing would come of it, of course. Brynn was too strong for that, but it made for tense Pack circles. She hated that she didn't have a firm place within the Pack other than the Alpha's sister. At one point, before her uncles had died and had still held the Pack ranks, her brothers had thought she'd be the Beta or even the Enforcer. Instead, she was...nothing.

Just herself, and not good enough in the moon goddess's eyes.

The others said it was because she was made for greater things, but now, she wasn't so sure.

If Finn had wanted her, had seen her as his, she'd be the Redwood Heir's mate.

And yet he'd stayed away.

And she was left alone.

Again.

Fate didn't make sense and left her wanting. Yet she couldn't wallow. Not anymore. She'd pick up the pieces that had been her soul and find a way to move on. Because the humans were coming, and the world was changing. She needed to protect her Pack because that was one thing she could do.

The only thing.

CHAPTER FIVE

The damned scent of her was going to kill him. One devastatingly seductive second at a time. Finn took a deep breath to calm himself and held back a curse. Inhaling a big gulp of air wasn't the best thing to do when it was Brynn's scent putting him on edge. Now he had her in his system, the tantalizing floral and spice wrapping around his cock until he was so hard he was afraid he'd fucking burst. He casually adjusted himself, aware that if her back hadn't been to him, she'd have tracked the movement. Then would have probably kicked him in said cock.

She seemed to hate him so much, and yet he couldn't stop thinking about her. Damn his Alpha and hers for putting them into this situation. Of course, if he'd fessed up to the fact that she made him hard and he couldn't stop thinking about her, maybe they'd have relented.

Or more than likely, they'd have told him to grow the fuck up and deal with the situation instead of hiding from it like a teenager.

If only she'd been his mate, then he'd feel free to act on his needs...her needs, as well. Because damn if he couldn't scent her arousal when the wind brushed along her skin just right. That soft skin that looked so fucking ready for him to bite and suckle, to rake his claws down as he pumped in and out of her sweet cunt, his dick filling her so full that neither of them would be able to walk for days afterward.

Fuuuuck.

Okay. Time to get his mind off that track. As it was, he wasn't sure he would be able to walk for much longer, considering his dick was so hard he practically had to waddle to keep up with her.

Because that was attractive and not at all conspicuous.

Way to blend in with the humans.

With a huge fucking hard-on for a woman who couldn't care less about him in her presence.

"What kind of coffee did you want?" Brynn asked, not bothering to look behind her. Her back was ramrod straight—like it had been since she'd walked into the shop and spotted him there. At least he'd been early this time.

Jesus, what the fuck was her problem? Yeah, they'd both been pulled into this job, but it wasn't as if it were the worst thing in the world. She *hated* him, and he had no idea what he'd done to deserve it.

Maybe she hated that she wanted him.

And he wasn't that much of an asshole to point it out to her.

At least not yet.

He saddled up next to her, knowing he was probably risking blood for getting so close, but damn it, they were supposed to be acting *normal*. Following her around while she stomped from place to place wasn't normal.

She stiffened at his side, but he didn't back down. Instead, he wrapped his arm around her shoulders, knowing he was risking more than blood this time. He leaned closer, aware that her wolf rose to the surface with each passing second. He could see it in her posture, her general being.

He was in her space, holding her too close when he *knew* she didn't want it, and he was a damned bastard for loving the feel of her by his side.

If only they were mates.

If only.

"Something cold, actually. It's hot outside." It was May in the Pacific Northwest. So it wasn't as hot as it was in the rest of the country, but he was burning up. That probably had more to do with the woman pressed up closely to his side than the temperature.

She turned her head so she faced him, a smile plastered on. Well, hell, this wasn't going to end well— not that he'd thought differently two seconds ago. "Two iced lattes, then," she said to the cashier even as she looked at him. "Wouldn't want you to overheat."

Her blue eyes brightened, a small sliver of gold rimming the outside, telling him her wolf was far closer to the surface than he'd thought. Shit. He hadn't wanted this. Brynn had amazing control of her wolf, and if his mere presence brought her to the edge due to anger, then he needed to take a step back and let her breathe. Because having her wolf come out and slash her claws across his chest for daring to touch her would have been *normal* inside a den. He frankly wouldn't have blamed her for it. But outside the den and in a world where every move they made was watched and studied, he knew he'd fucked up.

Carefully, he moved his arm away and took a step to the left. "Thank you," he said, his voice gruff. Her eyes tracked his movement and he saw her shoulders relax. Just two extra inches between them and she looked as if she could breathe again. He felt like a fucking tool for even forcing her to that line. He wasn't the type of man to encroach when not wanted, and yet he just had. There was no excuse other than he hadn't been thinking. Instead, he'd angered the woman he knew he needed to be friendly with and nothing more.

He pulled out his wallet and paid before she could. He heard the growl escape her lips and knew it was quiet enough that no one other than him would have been able to hear the soft sound. He leaned close to her ear but was careful not to touch her. "Sorry for touching you. You can pay next time."

There. He'd apologized. He'd do it again and in more detail later because he didn't like that he'd hurt her somehow. This anger had to come from somewhere, and he knew he wasn't perfect. Maybe he'd done something he wasn't aware of, but for the life of him, he couldn't think what it could possibly be. He'd fix it though. Because there was no way they could continue on like this and do work for their Pack if she couldn't even look at him without looking like she wanted to maim him.

"Thank you," she whispered back. A mere two words, and yet his body relaxed. His wolf stayed silent throughout the entire exchange. Yet that wasn't too out of the ordinary, considering his wolf was usually silent when he was around Brynn.

It was weird, but he didn't question it. Not when he knew things about his wolf wouldn't be like they were with the others. That was just how it was, and he'd learned to deal with it.

They waited in silence for their iced lattes, their bodies close to one another since space was lacking, but not touching. He could feel the heat of her and could still scent every inch of her, but he didn't move closer. He'd already crossed that line and refused to do it again.

He'd find out what made her tick though because damn it, he *liked* her. She was a strong wolf, one that protected what was hers. In any other world, they might have been friends, lovers, maybe something more. Now, though, he just wanted to walk into a room with her without her eyes narrowing and her body going tense.

It might be asking the impossible, but damn it, he was going to try.

The barista called their names, and Brynn stepped forward first, collecting both drinks. He let her gather his, not wanting to intrude on her space any more than he already had.

She handed him his drink, her fingers accidently brushing his in the process. She sucked in a breath, her eyes going wide and meeting his. He panted slightly and swallowed hard, not understanding what the fuck had just happened.

"Thank you," he growled out softly.

She pulled away, not quickly, but not slowly either. As if she were doing her hardest not to show her true emotions. Finn wondered what made Brynn Brentwood who she was.

He stepped aside and held out his arm, knowing she wouldn't take it but making it look as if he were pointing to the door. They wouldn't be sitting inside the coffee place that day, trying to make small talk while people stared at them. Instead, they were going for a walk and hitting a museum. Even after all these months of doing something similar to this, he still didn't know her well. They'd been chosen to go together in the first place because they blended well. They were both attractive and usually put people at ease if they tried—despite their dominance.

Now they had to convince the world they were harmless. At least for now. Honestly, Finn didn't think this approach would last long. There was only so much tension their world could take before something broke. The Packs would play the sweet and innocent wolves so the humans wouldn't fear them. But he had a feeling that one day, the humans would *need* to fear them. His father felt the same why, but they couldn't jump to that point yet. They had to go slow, integrate as much as they could.

Because his little brothers and his future nieces and nephews and cousins deserved to live in a world where they would be safe and not judged because of the blood in their veins. He'd do all in his power to protect his Pack from those that feared what they didn't understand.

Even learn to be near a woman who seemed to hate him and yet he craved like no other. If his wolf had even pushed him in the slightest, Finn would have thought Brynn was his mate. As it was, he'd never felt such a strong pull towards another, but his wolf hadn't uttered a single word. The damn thing just stayed silent, as if Brynn were just another wolf among the masses.

She led him to the outside patio and stopped on the sidewalk, taking a sip of her drink. His eyes followed the way her mouth sucked on the straw, her lips looking so fucking delectable he had to make sure he wasn't sporting wood.

Again.

This woman just might kill him in more ways than one before the day was out.

"So, the museum?" she asked, her voice husky. The effect had to be from the drink, not anything having to do with him.

She hated him, he told himself once again.

"Yeah. It's a quick walk from here so we don't have to move our cars." He wasn't sure he'd be able to handle being stuffed in a small car with her for too long. He'd break down and do something stupid like kiss her.

Then she'd geld him.

Not the most pleasant way to end the afternoon.

He cleared his throat. "Uh, so yeah, sorry again for crowding you in there. I'm just trying to figure out how to make this work. You know? Standing behind you and not talking wasn't enough, but putting my arm around your shoulder without asking probably pissed off your wolf. So for that, I'm sorry. I'll try not to invade your space."

There. That was civil enough.

Her eyes widened, and for a second, he thought he saw a flash of hurt cross her face, but it was gone so fast he wasn't sure what he'd seen. Why would she be hurt? He honestly didn't understand her, but he wanted to.

"I'm not a little wolf afraid of the big bad one," she said slowly as if she were being oh-so-careful with her words.

"I didn't say that. But I am a dominant wolf and so are you. I know better than to come at you from behind and touch you without permission. I didn't mean to fuck it up."

She blinked once, twice, then shook her head before looking around them both. No one was around them, he would have been able to scent them if there had been, so that was why he'd felt comfortable speaking the way he had, but it was always good to double check.

"It's fine. This won't be the last time we have to do this so..." she took a deep breath, as if steeling herself for the next words out of her mouth, "...so we need to make sure we can act like we're *normal* without stepping on each other's toes. So don't touch me and we should be fine."

He took a step back, his eyes wide. "We're wolves, Brynn. Touching is part of who we are."

Her lips thinned. "No, it's not part of who *we* are." She pointed between the two of them. "I don't need your touch to remind me you're a wolf, Finn. I don't need your touch to remind me you're the Heir either. So just keep your distance, and we will play nice with the world and show them we don't kill one another if we get a little testy."

"What the fuck is your problem?" he snapped, fed up.

She raised her chin, meeting his gaze. This time his wolf *did* react. It stormed to the front at the show of challenge. He clenched his jaw, holding himself back.

She moved her eyes slightly so they weren't looking at each other head on. His wolf didn't relent though. There had been a challenge there, like it or not. She might be one of the most dominant wolves he'd ever met, but she wasn't nearly as dominant as him.

His fists curled inward, his claws ready to come out. The man within was much stronger than the wolf, despite what others thought of him. Her wolf was right on the edge as well from the look in her eyes. Going at each other like this was the exact opposite of what they should be doing.

He was failing his Alpha, his family, his Pack by acting like an asshole, but damn it, she got under his skin in the worst ways possible sometimes.

"My problem is a little boy acting like he's the goddess's gift to the world. Just stay out of my way. When we get back, we'll find another pair to do this. It doesn't have to be us because I just can't. I can't act like nothing is wrong when you're around." Her mouth clamped shut and her eyes widened. Ah, she hadn't meant to say that last part.

Well, fuck it.

What was wrong with him? That's what he wanted to know. What had he done to put that look in her eyes? That tone in her voice?

"Look what we've got here, two wolves in one place. Shouldn't you be back at the zoo?" a man sneered as he made his way out of a dark alley, another man on his tail.

Brynn turned on her heel at the sound of the man's voice. She kept her claws in from what Finn could see, and he did the same. He stood at her back, keeping his attention on the surrounding areas. There might be more than just the two males in front of them. He might not know what the hell was going on between him and Brynn, but he, without a doubt, trusted her to protect herself *and* him in a fight.

That was just one more reason the woman confused him.

It wasn't the first time he'd heard the zoo comment. Hell, it wasn't even that original, but he despised humans who hated him without cause. It wasn't as if Finn and his family went on nightly hunts, changing humans and cackling like the Hollywood movies showed their kind to be. They didn't rely on the moon to shift. They didn't turn others unless they were their mates or in other dire circumstances. They weren't monsters on two legs without control.

They were families, children, and soldiers who protected their own.

And the human in front of him and others like him just didn't get it.

Finn was afraid they never would.

51

"Why don't you two run along now," Brynn said, her voice sickly sweet. He knew that voice. The sweeter she got in times like these, the more dangerous she was.

The second man grabbed his dick and wiggled his brows. "Why don't you get on your knees and tell me that."

Finn let out a slow growl, knowing he couldn't fucking kill this bastard right here. Not when other humans were gathering around, wondering what the wolves would do. Everything mattered. Every choice, every decision. Gutting the fool who dared threaten Brynn wouldn't help his Pack, but it might help his wolf.

"You're a fool," he muttered. "Just get out of our way. We're enjoying the nice day and we don't want any trouble."

Brynn's shoulders had stiffened at the man's taunt ever so slightly that Finn was sure he was the only one to see the movement. At Finn's words though, she relaxed into her ready-to-fight stance. It was hot as hell, but he wasn't about to lose focus.

"I'm going to ignore the fact you just threatened me like you did," Brynn continued. "We're not doing anything wrong, and I'm not in the mood to deal with a man who thinks he's tough by thinking it's okay to tell random women to get on their knees."

"You're not a woman. You're a dog," the first man snapped.

Finn tilted his head. "Then, with that logic, you want a dog around your cock. Seems to me you're the one with a problem." He took a step closer, watching the man's eyes widen. He heard both bastards' pulses race, but he did his best not to look menacing.

Normal.

That was the key word.

Only Finn didn't think there was a normal. Not anymore. Not that there ever had been one.

"Asshole."

Finn took another step so he was right by Brynn's side. Others surrounded them, but he only scented their fear and curiosity. The only threats were the two men in front of them. Brynn surprised the hell out of him by taking his hand.

Her palm was soft, softer than he thought possible. His pulse picked up at the contact, even though his attention was on the men in front of them.

"Goodbye." With that, she squeezed his hand, and he moved with her, walking to the side so the men didn't know what to do. The human males braced themselves, yet Finn and Brynn passed them, holding hands and not doing a single thing to threaten them. He had a feeling in the world of technology and instant communication, someone had shot a video of the altercation; there was no getting out of that. But all they would see was a man and woman trying to get by two men who'd come at them. They hadn't done a single thing wrong and hadn't responded to the threats.

He prayed that would be enough. Because if it wasn't? Then acting normal wouldn't be enough. Instead, they'd have to take the next step, and Finn wasn't sure the world was ready for that.

Brynn released his hand as soon as they turned the corner, and he immediately felt the loss. "Assholes," she muttered.

He snorted, even though the adrenaline rushing through his system hadn't abated. His wolf wanted a fight, and it hadn't gotten one. It would have to deal though because he'd already fought with Brynn enough. It didn't escape his attention that they hadn't finished their argument from earlier, but he wasn't in the mood to deal with that. Not after what had just happened. Going against instinct and not pummeling the man for daring to even think about hurting Brynn had been hard as hell. He didn't have the energy not to do something stupid like pull Brynn close and kiss her until they were both out of breath and gasping each other's names as they came.

"Ready for the museum?" he asked, his voice a harsh growl.

She turned to face him, her brows raised. "You still want to do this?"

"We have to," he bit out. "I don't care if we're fighting with each other, we're here for our Packs. They come before any of that shit."

She let out a breath. "I get it. And for what it's worth, thank you for not killing those assholes."

He snorted. "Killing them would have been easy," he muttered, aware they shouldn't be discussing killing outside on a street. "They threatened you. They deserved worse."

She swallowed hard before turning away from them. "I could have handled them on my own."

"I know." That was one of the many things he admired about her. "But you didn't have to, and frankly, I'm glad neither one of us was alone just then. It's good we were together. If not, we might have forgotten to rein it in and done something stupid like claw that fucking smirk off the bastard's face."

She gave him a look out of the side of her eye that he couldn't figure out. "That's true." She shook her now mostly warm latte. Ice didn't last long in this heat. "I'm done with this. You?" He nodded, not in the mood for something sweet that wasn't the woman in front of him. *Dangerous.* "Okay, then. Let's go look at some artwork and pretend that I'm not older than half of it." Her mouth quirked in a semblance of a smile.

He threw back his head back and laughed. "You're not that old, Brynn."

"I'm older than you, pup."

Pup. That had to be part of the hatred, but damn if he cared right then. She confused the hell out of him, but since she wasn't physically pushing him away, he'd take what he could get for the time being.

"Whatever. You can show me what paintings are what. My uncle Reed tried to show me the world of art and I got distracted by shiny things like running and screaming at the top of my lungs to scare Brie." He grinned and she rolled her eyes. Progress.

"I don't know that much," she said with a shrug. "Unlike you Redwoods, we Talons didn't get out much." Her features clouded and he wanted to curse himself for mentioning happier times as a child. Her childhood had sucked. Though *sucked* wasn't a strong enough word. However, he wasn't going to get into that. Not then.

"Then I guess this will be an experience for the both of us," he said softly.

She met his gaze, blinked. "I guess so."

He swallowed hard, not knowing why he was acting this way. He'd found other women attractive before, of course. He'd been with women in the past. It wasn't like he was a thirty-something-year-old virgin. But he'd never felt this kind of an urge with another woman before. And if his wolf had even felt an inkling of what he did right then, he'd have said Brynn was his mate.

And if he'd been any other man, if she'd been any other woman, he'd have said screw it all to fate and would have taken her. Damn their future potential mates. But he wasn't that man, and she wasn't that woman. Instead, he'd walk with her inside that museum and do his best to try and be her...what?

Friend? Ally? He didn't know, but fighting with her was killing him, and he wasn't sure he could keep doing it and not make a mistake.

"You should be fucking killed and shot on sight. Fucking animals."

Finn turned on his heel at the sound of the same man from before. It seemed he and his friend had found their balls and followed Brynn and Finn to the steps of the museum. Damn it. This was not how it was supposed to go. How were they going to look like nothing was wrong and prove that wolves could be part of society like they'd been for generations—if only in secret—if random humans with too much hate in their hearts and souls kept coming at them?

This part of the Alphas' plan would end swiftly if Finn and Brynn didn't find another way to deal with this.

"Go away," Finn growled, taking Brynn's hand. She stiffened and he wanted to kick himself. He'd done it instinctually, wanting her touch so he could make sure she was by his side in case things went to hell. Yet he'd touched her when she'd told him not to, when he'd promised her he'd wouldn't. It didn't matter she'd done the same damn thing not ten minutes earlier by taking his hand. The woman tore him up inside and he didn't know how to fix it.

The man who'd grabbed himself before but had spoken the least tugged on his friend's arm. "Let's go, man." It seemed the little fucker wasn't too keen on getting his ass kicked by a couple of wolves far stronger than him. Smart.

Both humans sniffed then walked away, leaving Brynn and Finn alone once again.

Brynn let out a breath, her hand still in his. "I think we should just go. That was a little too much for one day, don't you think?"

Finn inhaled through his nose, catching her scent one more time. Instead of answering, he tugged her toward the alley a few feet to the side of them and pushed her back against the wall. They hadn't had time to gather an audience like they had the first time, so no one would have seen him pull her close to him, thankfully.

"What the fuck are you doing?" she snapped. Her wolf glowed in her eyes, but he scented her arousal, tasted it on his tongue. She *wanted* him.

"Doing what we should have done a year ago," he growled.

Then he did something spectacularly brilliant and idiotic at the same time.

He kissed her.

He had his hands on hers, pinning her to the wall. The bricks had to be digging into her back, but he knew she'd take it. Then maybe she'd pin him later and let him feel that pain, as well. She gasped against his mouth then opened, her tongue sliding along the seam of his lips. He groaned, tangling his tongue with hers, her sweet and exotic taste bursting on his tongue. He rocked against her, his erection pressing firmly into her flat belly. She wrapped a leg around his thigh, pulling him closer, making him want to beg for more. When she arched against him, her nipples pressing into his chest, he groaned into her mouth. He wanted to tangle his fingers in her hair, wanted to run his hands down her sides, cup her breasts, undo her pants and feel her wet heat.

Yet he didn't do any of that.

Not then.

Instead, he kissed her harder, wanting every ounce of her.

Before he could take a breath, she slashed his hands with her claws and he winced, pulling back ever so slightly. She pushed at his chest and he moved back more.

Fuck.

She'd kissed him back, had pressed her body to his, but she'd pushed him at the end. He'd moved because she'd pushed, but he'd fucked up. He opened his mouth to apologize, not knowing what the fuck had just happened, but before he could get out a word, she slapped him.

Hard.

Claws and all.

The metallic stench of blood filled his nostrils and he knew she'd cut his face as well as his hands.

"Why?" she gasped, her eyes wide. "*Why?*"

CHAPTER SIX

"Why?" Brynn pleaded, her heart in her throat. *"Why?"*

She staggered from the wall, careful not to touch him. Just one taste, one touch, and she was addicted. He reached for her, then must have thought better of it because he dropped his hand. Her wolf begged for him while the woman wanted to rage in agony and sweet release.

He'd kissed her.

He'd freaking kissed her.

He wasn't supposed to kiss her. He was supposed to keep his distance and make it easier for her to die slowly inside. He didn't want her; he'd proven that over the past year by looking right through her as nothing but a woman, wolf, a fighter—not a potential mate.

Yet he'd pressed her against the wall and kissed her like he'd meant it, like he wanted something more than a mere kiss. Though that had been no mere kiss. That had been...*everything.*

She'd always known when Finn wanted something he'd go for it all—as if he couldn't help putting everything into it, putting his whole body, his wolf, his *tongue*. She'd heard enough stories from women who'd been in his bed. While she hadn't clawed their eyes out for daring to touch what should have been hers, she'd listened to their tales of his prowess. Finn wasn't a gentle lover, but he was a caring one. He fucked like he had a purpose, and made sure every woman in his bed got off until she couldn't walk away easily. Because it was Finn who always did the walking away—apparently, on the hunt for a mate.

Too bad he'd missed what was right in front of him on that search.

From the way he'd kissed just then though, she had a feeling he'd been holding back from those women. Sure, he hadn't been gentle, hadn't been easy, but there was something *more* in the way he'd pressed her hard against the wall. She knew she'd have bruises from his hold, from the brick at her back, and she *relished* it. She wanted to have his mark at her hips, at her neck. She wanted to show the world that Finn had her, and then she'd mark him as well to show those women that she had *him*.

Only that wouldn't happen.

A sob caught in her throat and she forced a growl to cover it up. From the look in Finn's eyes, she hadn't covered it up well enough.

Damn it.

It wasn't supposed to be like this. Fate and mating weren't supposed to be this difficult. Of course, she knew that was a crock considering how her friends and her brother had mated. Nothing that truly mattered was ever easy, but damn it, none of them had ever had this...this pain...this lack of anything tangible.

"Why?" she repeated, forcing her heart to slow. Thankfully, her voice didn't crack, and she held the tears at bay.

"Because I wanted to. I needed to. I thought you were of the same mind." Finn genuinely looked confused. Even with his chest heaving as if he needed to catch his breath, he looked so damn sexy.

He shouldn't. She should hate him for making her feel like she was nothing, for making her think that she had a future filled with the pain of seeing him every day and not being able to have him.

"You know nothing." She swallowed hard. "You kissed me because you wanted to? Or because you were bored? Because you've never done anything like that before, and we've been together, *alone*, countless times in the past."

And every single time they had, she'd been reduced to a twisty and tattered version of herself. For that, she would hate him for eternity if she could. She'd spent her life trying to figure out how to become the person she needed to be for her Pack. She never wanted to go back to the heaping mess of a wolf she'd been at the hands of her father. Her brothers and cousins might have told her that she'd been strong under his care, but she didn't believe them. Not when she'd cried more often than not. She might have done her best to keep the tears in and hide any that escaped so the others—and her—wouldn't be hurt even more, but it had never been enough.

The man in front of her had slowly chipped away at the woman she'd become, and she would never forgive him for that. Her mind needed to be on the task at hand and not at what could have been or even what was. The future of her Pack, of every Pack out there, rested on her shoulders. She couldn't falter because her wolf wanted a wolf that didn't know what to do with her.

"I wasn't bored," Finn growled. "Fuck that. I've scented your arousal every time I'm near. Don't tell me you couldn't tell I've been hard as fuck when I'm close to you."

She sucked in a breath, her face heating. Damn it. She wasn't a blushing virgin, but Finn brought out the worst in her. She *knew* she'd been turned on in his presence, but she'd done her best to hide it. No one else had been able to tell, that much she was sure of, so why the hell could he sense it? And no, she hadn't noticed his hard-ons. In fact, she'd done her best to keep her line of sight away from his dick. One look and she'd be a goner. Considering she'd felt the bulge against her belly when he'd pressed her into the wall, she'd have probably fallen to her knees in praise if she'd ever dared to look.

Damn Finn Jamenson and his dick.

"Fuck you, Finn. I might have been turned on, but for all you know, it's because I was thinking about the man I had in my bed the night before. Don't be so self-centered and think it's all for you." Lies, but damn it, if he hadn't acknowledged the need for a potential mate, then she wasn't going to let him get any closer than he was. There was no way she'd be able to breathe if she did.

Finn's eyes narrowed. "You had a man in your bed last night and yet you wrapped your leg around my thigh today?"

She snarled. "What if I did? It's not like you're a saint. I'm not mated." Pain. Shatter. Agony. "I can do whatever the fuck I want. Get off it, Finn. It's never happening again."

It couldn't. Not if she wanted to remain sane. Her wolf *knew* Finn's didn't feel the same thing she did. It wasn't a lack of communication, or her being an overemotional woman. Finn's wolf hadn't *once* reached out for Brynn's wolf. The mating urge had kicked in for Brynn, but it hadn't for Finn. That was clear as day.

Fate had fucked up and given her a mate who couldn't feel the same potential bond she did.

Maybe the torture she'd endured at the hands of her father and uncles had fucked her up so badly she didn't know what she was feeling. Or maybe fate was punishing her for her hand in their deaths. Gideon might have dealt the final blow, but she had blood on her hands, as well.

Fate had once punished the entire Pack for her father's actions by not allowing a single mating to take place in over fifteen years. It had taken the love of a Redwood princess and a broken Talon wolf to piece the ties of mating within the Pack back together.

Maybe the punishment wasn't quite over.

Maybe Brynn needed to feel the pain of loss and a never-ending example of what happened when one crossed the paths of fate and destiny.

Whatever it was, she'd endure it. She had before, and she would again. But she couldn't do it if she had to see Finn at her side and never be able to touch him. Or worse, touch him and know it would never go past that.

A touch.

A caress.

Never anything more.

He took a step forward, and she froze. What was he doing? He reached out and tucked a strand of her hair behind her ear. She could scent him; that spiciness that made her think of exotic, dark things that she shouldn't be thinking of.

"I'm sorry," he whispered.

She blinked, a jagged tear slicing through her once again.

He was *sorry*?

Sorry?

Of course, he was fucking sorry. What else would he be?

"Sorry?" she croaked. She cleared her throat and raised her chin. She was better than this, better than a broken shell of a woman who couldn't hide the pain inside. "Sorry for what? Kissing me? Or thinking that I could ever want you?"

Lie.

All lies.

But what was the alternative?

The words burned on her tongue, and the shock in Finn's eyes at her tone—or maybe it was her words—told her she'd gone too far. But she didn't care anymore. Not when he'd been hurting her for the past year.

He couldn't kiss her and make her want more when she knew they'd never have it. She wouldn't let herself live half a life when her wolf craved more.

It wasn't fair to either of them.

And, goddess, if he were to ever find his real mate?

Bile rose in her throat.

No, she wouldn't think about that.

Ever.

"You sure like those barbs when you're pressed into a corner."

She snarled again. "Then don't push me. Don't touch me. This will never happen again." It couldn't. "Now, we're standing in the middle of an alley all alone instead of doing our job. I'd say that's the real fucked up situation here. So let's get back out there and act like we're fine and that I don't want to kick you in the balls because you piss me the fuck off."

That was true, though she really wanted to do something else with his balls first.

Damn it.

Mind. Gutter. Bad.

Finn flared his nostrils then raised his chin. "Fine. We'll head back like we planned but know this, Brynn Brentwood—we aren't through. Far from it."

And that's what scared her. Because she didn't know why he'd kissed her. Sure, he'd said it was because he'd wanted to. But what did that mean? She couldn't be with a man that she wanted forever and know that he'd only want her for a tumble. She didn't hate herself that much. So where he might want to continue this line of conversation, she knew she couldn't. Not when she wanted to run her hands through his hair and tug. She missed the longer length where she knew she'd be able to get a good grip, but this shorter version would be good enough. That was, of course, if she let herself fantasize. Which she wouldn't. Not in the slightest.

"Move out of my way before I move you myself."

Finn raised a brow. Why did the man have to look sexy doing that? "That doesn't sound like cooperation between Packs to me."

"You just shoved me against a wall and put your tongue down my throat. I think we're through with cooperation."

"Actually, that sounds like perfect cooperation to me. Let's do it again."

Brynn's hands shook. She'd heard of this Finn— the sarcastic one that made people smile by just being himself. But she hadn't seen it before. Or maybe she had, but she'd been so clouded by her own pain and worries she'd missed it. However, she couldn't deal with this right then. In fact, she couldn't deal with it ever. Maybe if she hadn't been bleeding inside, she would have enjoyed the man in front of her and his humor. Instead, all she saw was a mistake.

And that killed her one exquisitely painful inch at a time.

Enough of that. Seriously. She had a job to do, and her brain wasn't in the right place.

"You done acting like a little pup who didn't get his treat?" Better to put their age difference in the forefront. That would help push him away.

He shook his head, his hair sliding over his eyes before he pushed it back again. He might have cut some of it, but he hadn't lost all of its length. Damned man looked good no matter what he did.

"Let's go."

"Fine with me." She moved past him, careful not to brush against him but doing her best not to look like she was being careful. Gideon needed to find a new wolf to mingle with the humans because doing this with Finn had turned her into a damn teenager worried about study hall and passing notes about boys. She wasn't sure she could take much more of this. She'd turned into a complete ball of angst, rather than merely the mess she was now.

As soon as she stepped out from the alley, she took a deep breath, trying to clear her senses of everything Finn. It wasn't easy to do seeing how he was right behind her, taking up too much space. She'd been an idiot to think she could help her Pack, her people, by acting like everything was normal. It was so far from normal she wasn't even sure she remembered what normalcy was.

"Back to the dens, then?" he said from behind her.

"Yeah. We'll do better next time." She paused. "With different people. The world needs to know more than just the two of us."

The sound of a photo shutter hit her ears and she raised her chin toward the noise, doing her best to look calm.

"I heard it, too," he whispered. A pause. "And yeah, next time we'll go out with others. Maybe Max would want to hang out with me."

Her cousin Max was the most easygoing wolf she knew. He'd escaped through their version of hell a better man than she could have thought possible.

"You and Max have worked together with the council in the past." Not a question, but he answered anyway.

"Yeah. Our Packs have worked together well for thirty years now," he said softly. It stung that the two of them couldn't, but she knew she couldn't care for much longer.

"Where do you think that picture is going?" she asked, ignoring his last statement. "A curious human? Media? The government? I hate not knowing. But I also hate that we have to live with it so others learn not to fear us." She smiled softly at a small child who waved at them. The little girl's mother met Brynn's eyes and paled before tucking her child closer.

It hurt, the slice of familiar pain that told her that, yet again, she wasn't good enough. That she was something to fear, or worse, pity.

"She just doesn't understand," Finn said softly, moving closer to her so no one could overhear. "They will, though. What we're doing matters. We aren't monsters. They'll see that."

She closed her eyes before taking a deep breath. When she opened them, the sun hadn't faded, hadn't burst into a thousand flames. Instead, time moved forward as it always had—ever slowly toward an absolution that would never come.

"I'm sorry, again," he whispered, and she wanted to kick him. Again.

"Don't be," she snapped. "It was a mistake that will never happen again. We won't even talk about it. It's like it never happened."

"But it did happen, Brynn. We should talk about why."

"We really shouldn't. So get over yourself, Finn, and leave me alone. Got it?"

He didn't touch her—he'd told her he wouldn't—but he was close enough that she could practically feel every inch of him. "I've got it just fine, princess."

"Thanks, *prince*." He was just as much royalty as she—even more so since he held the title while she had nothing.

He snorted then stiffened before moving faster than she'd ever seen him move. Brynn went on alert, following him instinctually before letting her mind process her thoughts.

A car came out of nowhere, barreling toward them. She moved faster, putting her wolf in the action, knowing she needed to follow Finn. He wasn't moving out of the way of the car. Instead, he moved toward the little girl from before who had just stepped off the curb.

Brynn screamed as Finn tucked the little girl close and took the brunt of the car's assault on himself. The car skidded as Finn rolled over the top of it, landing on his feet, the little girl safely tucked in his arms.

The car sped off, leaving an array of screaming and shell-shocked humans.

Finn hadn't gone wolf, instead, had moved with supernatural speed to save a human girl. He'd been hit by a car but landed on his feet with only a few cuts to show for it.

So much for blending in with the humans.

"Did you see that?"

"He saved that little girl!"

"What just happened?"

"I've never seen anyone move like that!"

"I thought wolves would have just let her die."

"What a hero!"

The scent of burned rubber mixed with the tangy scent of spilled blood. Her wolf raged at the smell, but she pushed it back, knowing she couldn't full-on shift in public with so many eyes on her. This man, this wolf, had almost died protecting a little girl who'd run out into the street when she shouldn't have. As it was, Brynn's whole body threatened to shake from adrenaline.

She'd almost lost Finn just then.

Almost lost him without ever having him.

Another photo shutter sounded and she moved forward, trying to ignore the calls for her name, the calls for what had happened right in front of her. She'd deal with the humans and the public's need to know every single little thing in a moment. First, she needed to put her hands on Finn to make sure he was truly alive. It didn't matter that he was moving and speaking slowly to the little girl in his arms. All that mattered was that he was hurt, and her wolf needed to protect above all else. She was a fucking dominant shifter, and she knew her role, her duties. To *protect*. To serve her Alpha.

And now, to ensure Finn was safe.

Damn it.

She didn't want that last one, but it seemed her wolf wouldn't let her out of it. "Finn."

He looked up at her for a moment, his wolf in his eyes before he blinked it away. "I'm fine." He kept his voice light, and she knew it was for the benefit of the little girl in his arms. "And so is Lacey. Right, honey?"

Lacey nodded, completely enraptured by the perfect specimen that was Finn. Brynn couldn't blame the little girl. She was pretty sure her face had looked like that once or twice—wide eyes and her mouth agape, even with a slight blush on her cheeks.

"Lacey!" The same mother who had looked so scared of Brynn before ran toward the group of them, tears running down her cheeks. "Baby!"

"She's okay, ma'am," Finn said softly, his voice gruff. "The car never touched her. I promise you."

"I don't hurt, Mommy. It was like a hug."

The mom pulled her daughter close, her gaze darting over the little girl's body. "I...I..."

A siren pierced the distance. "I think that's an ambulance coming," Brynn added in. The mother looked at her quickly, then back at her daughter. Brynn didn't blame the woman for wanting to keep her eyes on Lacey at all times. That had been too close for comfort. "We can have her checked out just in case."

"Thank you," the mother whispered. "Thank you for saving my baby. She just ran out into the street, and that car came out of nowhere."

Brynn met Finn's gaze. The car that had hit him and proceeded to drive away hadn't been there by accident. She'd seen the driver and his passenger. The familiar faces of the men who had accosted them before burned bright in her mind. Lacey had almost died because she'd been in the wrong place at the wrong time. If she hadn't darted out into the street when she had, the car would have kept going and would have plowed into Brynn and Finn. Of course, they would have jumped out of the way, and with their shifter reflexes should have probably been fine, but it was still scary.

And ominous.

Those men had tried to kill them, and she only knew they hated her and Finn for being wolves. That kind of bigotry wasn't new, but it was getting more and more dangerous to be outside the den.

Not good for what she and Finn were trying to accomplish with being out in public like they were.

Brynn moved closer to Finn, her hand out for him. He put his palm to hers and stood in one swift move. She knew he could have gotten up on his own, but he'd let her help him. That was no small feat for such a dominant wolf. It just showed her she didn't know Finn at all. He had a few gashes on his face and he'd shredded part of his right arm and leg, but it was already healing. She met his gaze and he nodded. They needed to get out of there before people truly saw him heal. Sure, humans knew part of the mystery of wolves, but the two of them didn't need to put on a show. Well, any more than they already had.

People had shot video of the accident, she was sure of it, as she'd felt the cameras on them when they'd just been standing outside the alley. Animals outside the zoo were much more interesting to look at than trying to hunt for dens that humans had once hidden from.

"Thank you," the mother said softly, her gaze intently on Finn. Others came toward them even as the paramedics looked Lacey over. The police were looking around and would be asking questions soon. Brynn recognized two of the officers as pro-shifter so she knew they wouldn't be detained. It might not have been her or Finn behind the wheel, but it wasn't that far-fetched that others would want to blame the two of them for the hit and run. After all, the humans driving the car had been out for Finn and Brynn, she was sure of it.

"Thank you for saving my daughter," the mother said again, tears in her voice.

Finn nodded, his face solemn. "I'm glad I could help."

A paramedic looked toward Finn and raised a brow. "You need a bandage for that?" the man asked, curiosity in his tone.

Brynn stepped forward, holding out her hand. "That would be great. I'll help him though so you can take care of the little girl." She met the man's eyes then purposely looked around them. They'd gathered a crowd, and while the Packs had wanted them to blend in, this wasn't the best way to do it.

"Sure. No problem." The paramedic handed her a few bandages and shrugged. She wasn't sure that was going with protocol, but she didn't care. Not when Finn was still bleeding and she needed to get them both out of there. Now.

"Thanks." She turned to Finn. "Ready?" One of the cops nodded at her and she sighed. "Let's get this over with."

Finn tilted his head, and she knew he was confused. She couldn't act on character because she didn't *know* how to act around him. He was hurt, and she needed to take care of him. But she also couldn't show that she *needed* that. It was a mess, and now she had to play nice for the humans.

Things had gone to hell, and it was only the beginning.

And for some reason, she felt like it would always be the beginning. At least until something happened that made more than one wolf bleed.

And when that day came, she wasn't sure what she would do.

CHAPTER SEVEN

Finn ran a hand over his face, wincing when a twinge ached across his side. He'd almost fully healed by the time he and Brynn had left the curious cops and bystanders and made their way back to the respective dens. He just had a few bruises that would take a couple of days to go away. His healing worked on the major things first, then the smaller ones—a perk of being a wolf.

"You need to see Hannah or Mark?" Maddox asked. Maddox was his uncle and former Omega. Or really, his Omega in truth since the Pack was still in flux. Hannah, his aunt, was the former Healer with his brother Mark learning his new powers right beside her. His other brother, Drake, sat by Maddox, a frown on his face. Drake was the new Omega, but even in his twenties, far too young in Finn's opinion to deal with the weight of the world that the Omega had to deal with on a daily basis.

Finn shook his head. "I'm fine. They don't need to waste their energy on a few bruises." He ran his hand over his side but didn't wince this time. That had to be some form of progress.

Maddox raised a brow. The man didn't speak as much as his other uncles, but when he did, it meant something. Uncle Maddox had been through hell and back, coming through it with the love of a woman that provided his anchor to the world. Without Ellie, Finn had a feeling Maddox would have succumbed to the pain and overwhelming emotions that came with being the Omega of a large Pack in the center of a war. The mating bond with Ellie had saved Maddox's life.

That was one more reason Finn was glad Maddox still held some bonds to the Pack through being an Omega. Mark wouldn't be able to handle every emotion—good or bad—on his own. Finn had no idea how Maddox had done it all those years ago, but now Mark at least had someone to rely on when things got tricky. And in a time where no one knew what the next step would be, and everyone's lives were in danger because the humans were too unpredictable, Finn was so freaking relieved Maddox was there to pick up the slack.

All of his family had a backup power holder because of the shift in hierarchy. He wasn't sure how long the older generation would keep the powers they had and the connections they shared, but they were needed. The moon goddess could see their Pack needed the help with what was to come. The Talons didn't have that option, but they also had wolves with a century of living under their belt. Finn's generation didn't have that yet. In fact, he and his father were the only ones within the Redwoods without a counterpart. It made sense, as there was only one Alpha. One whose word was law. Finn had no children, no other connections to share. So he was the Heir.

As he'd been since he was three years old.

Maddox put his hand on Finn's shoulder, breaking Finn from the memories of screams and fire.

"You're projecting so hard right now, that it doesn't take an Omega to know you're in pain." Maddox sighed. "And I'm not talking about the bruises."

Finn shrugged. "I'm fine."

"You're lying." Maddox hadn't always been this blunt. In fact, if Finn didn't know any better, he would have sworn that tone had come from his uncle Adam. The Enforcer of the Pack used to be a growly asshole. Now, he was a growly asshole who smiled when his mate and children were near.

"I'll be fine," Finn said, truthfully. "How's that?"

Drake snorted. "That'll have to do, won't it?"

Finn flipped Drake off then sat back in his chair. After the cops had been dealt with, he'd come back home and had wanted to sleep off whatever the fuck had happened with Brynn. Of course, he should have known that wouldn't be happening. Maddox had been waiting on the doorstep with Drake by his side. Normally the two would have just walked right inside and waited for Finn there. But since Charlotte also lived with Finn and she was Maddox's daughter, Finn figured there had to be some boundaries in place. Charlotte wasn't home, so Maddox had waited for Finn to arrive.

And as soon as Finn had let the pair inside, he'd been forced to tell them exactly what had happened with the humans and the accident that wasn't quite an accident. Finn had left out the part where he'd pressed Brynn up against the wall and kissed her like he'd never kissed a woman before. That part was just for him.

Though he had a feeling Maddox was here for *exactly* that part. Any one of his family members could have stopped by to hear firsthand what had happened outside the den. Finn would be talking to his father about it again soon anyway.

Instead, the two Omegas of the Pack had shown up on his doorstep with serious faces to match the serious business at hand.

"Tell me what happened with Brynn."

Finn sat back, his eyes narrowing at his uncle. "Beyond the accident and the asshole humans who followed us around?"

Maddox let out a sigh while Drake shifted uncomfortably in his chair. Finn wasn't doing a good enough job hiding his emotions if he was making his brother feel like this, but damn it, he couldn't control himself every moment of every day. He'd done a piss poor job of controlling himself around Brynn earlier, and he wouldn't blame her for never speaking to him again.

Only he wanted to see her again. Wanted to speak to her. Wanted to kiss her again.

And that was fucking dangerous.

"Finn."

The knowing tone in Maddox's voice set Finn's teeth on edge. He didn't want to talk about it. Didn't want to think about it. But whom else would he speak to? His father? No. That would just fuck things up since Brynn was the Talon Princess. No matter how hard Kade tried to be only a father, there were times he had to be only the Alpha. Finn never begrudged his father for that, but it didn't make things easy.

"I don't want to talk about it," he growled lowly. As Heir, he might outrank the other two in the room, but right then, they were his Omegas, his family. He wouldn't be able to hide from them for long. And honestly, he wasn't sure he should.

Maddox sighed then leaned back in his chair. "You know, when you were younger, I would have thought you were the next Omega."

Finn sat straighter, startled. "Huh? I'm the Heir. The firstborn. The others had options when it came to what the moon goddess would bless them with, but I always had the same path as my father."

Maddox raised a brow. "The way you put that makes me think it's something else we need to talk about."

Drake mumbled an assent, and Finn wanted to crawl in a hole and hide. Oh sure, he could fight like no other and was one of the most dominant wolves out there, but get him in a room where he was forced to talk about his feelings for long stretches of time and he wanted to hide.

"What did you mean about me being an Omega?" he asked, trying to stay on topic. Or at least on one of the many topics filling the room. His uncle Maddox was like that, poking at different ideas until one latched on and Finn was able to finally share *something*. It might not be everything, might not be the most important thing, but it was *something*.

"You were always so intuitive," Maddox continued, shelving the more difficult topic. Or maybe not so much, considering what they were discussing. "You were too young to remember, but I was the first to babysit you alone while Melanie and Kade took some time for themselves."

Finn snorted. "I don't remember exactly, but Mom and Dad mentioned the horror of your experience."

Drake snickered. "Horror sounds right. Having to deal with Finn's diapers? No thanks."

Finn flipped his little brother off. "I wasn't too young to deal with your diapers, little Omega. Talk about horror."

Maddox laughed then ran a hand over his jaw. "That was part of it. But I think the horror came from how sticky you were. I have no idea how you got so dirty so quickly, but you freaking loved getting jam hands and wiping them on my shirt...and my face."

Finn grinned. "I'd apologize, but I think I was freaking adorable."

Maddox rolled his eyes. "Oh, you were that. We hadn't adopted Gina or Mark or even Parker and Charlotte into the family yet, so you were the first grandchild. Everyone doted on you and wanted to watch you when Kade took Mel out on that getaway they so desperately needed. I don't even know why I offered, I think most people were too busy with things that couldn't be put aside." He paused, his eyes going dark. "I wasn't in the best place then. I didn't have Ellie, and I was fighting with North." Maddox's twin. "But I came over to your parents' home and watched you. You destroyed most of the house since I apparently had forgotten what it was like to watch a baby. Considering I helped raise Cailin, I don't know why I'd forgotten. She was even more of a terror."

Finn and Drake laughed, even as they looked over their shoulders. Cailin was far younger than her six brothers and might be a terror, but she would kick their asses if she heard them say it.

"So we hung out, and you got jam and who knows what else all over me. But when I wanted to recede to the darkness, you didn't let me." Maddox set his jaw. "You put your hand on my cheek and met my gaze. In that moment, I couldn't hide from who I was, what I was becoming. If you hadn't been set on that path you speak of, I would have thought you were destined to work by my side." He met Finn's eyes. "The goddess has surprised us before."

That was an understatement.

Finn let out a shaky breath. "Why are you telling me this?"

"Because despite what the moon goddess gave you when you were three, you are not *only* the Heir. You are a man as well, one who is so intuitive you could have been the Omega or any other power within the Pack. Hell, you could have been a fantastic soldier without a power with the way you can see into others without much thought."

"It's true," Drake said quietly. "I can feel it in the bonds." His younger brother grimaced. "I try not to look too hard at the bonds because some things are private, and if I dive too deep, I might not ever come out. But when I see yours, I see the strength we need as our leader, but also the compassion it takes to be more."

Finn cleared his throat, not knowing what to say.

"And sometimes I feel as though the bond isn't as strong as the others," Drake said then clamped his mouth shut.

Finn blinked. "What does that mean?"

Maddox met Drake's eyes and shook his head.

"What? Don't keep secrets."

Maddox let out a breath. "When you came back from near death, you told us once your wolf was different."

Finn froze.

"Sometimes we feel that along the bonds. Or, at least what we think that is. It could be nothing. It could be that Drake and I are working too hard on one bond at a time. It could be that you're good at hiding what you feel, and that's fine, too. It could be nothing, Finn."

He swallowed hard. He'd always known he was broken. Or had once been broken and sealed back together. But what if Hannah had missed something when she'd Healed him? What if she'd forgotten a key piece?

What if the broken pieces shattered under the touch of a woman he didn't understand—the strength of a soul so vivid that he could taste it on the wind?

"I can't talk about it," Finn whispered. "Not right now." He ran a hand over his face, knowing he was ducking the important things. But he couldn't put it into words. There was something missing, and he had no idea if it was connected to the intensity that came from being around Brynn, but he didn't want to voice his thoughts and ruin it all before it had begun. He could just be overreaching, but he didn't know anymore.

Maddox frowned at him then reached out and patted Drake's knee when the younger man opened his mouth to speak. "We won't push you. Not yet. I pushed my brothers at times when it was warranted, but I might have hurt them in the process. I won't do that to you."

"But I might," Drake said softly. "To save you? To make you feel whole? I'd do anything, Finn. You're my brother. Remember that."

Finn swallowed hard, knowing he wouldn't be able to hide everything for much longer. He'd tell them about Brynn, about his wolf, about his path...about everything. When he could. There was no *if* anymore. He couldn't hold it in for too much longer.

"I'll remember," he whispered then cleared his throat. "While you're here," he said, changing the subject, "I'll let you know a little bit of what I'm going to talk to Dad about."

"Other than the events of earlier?" Maddox asked.

Finn nodded. "Yeah. The outside world is one issue. But inside the Pack? We have issues of our own. I know as Betas, Nick and Jasper are working with the Pack to ensure they are functioning on a day-to-day level. But with all that's happened in the past year, I feel as though we're on an edge I can't quite place. Our wolves are worried and trying to figure out how to live and not go crazy while stuck inside the den."

Maddox frowned. "I've been feeling that...unease, as well. I know Jasper has since we've discussed it. Pack circles and events within the den wards can only do so much."

"We're going to have to find a way to keep the health of the Pack priority—not just their safety."

Maddox quirked his mouth up in a smile. "You sound like your father."

Finn raised his chin, the compliment washing over his skin.

"We're having a family meeting tomorrow morning. We'll find a way."

The front door opened, and Finn turned to see Charlotte walking in, a frown on her face, and Bram, a mid-level ranking wolf on her tail. He had his hands in tight fists at his sides, the darkness of his skin holding the sheen of perspiration.

Charlotte froze mid-step as soon as she looked up. Bram didn't run into her as he'd had his attention on the three men in the room from the start.

"Dad? What are you doing here?"

Maddox stood up, his brows raised. He folded his arms over his chest, and Finn held back a groan. He didn't know what was going on between Bram and Charlotte, but having an angry dad in the room probably wouldn't help.

"I needed to talk with Finn." His gaze moved to Bram. "Bram."

"Sir." The deep growl of Bram's voice didn't sound like he was afraid of the power in the room. In fact, it sounded like he was on edge.

This wasn't going to end well, and he wasn't in the mood to mess with Charlotte. She needed her privacy—even if Maddox didn't always see that. Not to mention, Finn needed time on his own right then. He had to formulate a plan and decompress after getting hit by a freaking car.

"Thanks for stopping by, Maddox and Drake. I'll see you both at the meeting."

Maddox didn't move his gaze from Bram, yet Charlotte didn't move from standing in front of him. Finn wasn't sure what was going on, but it was their business unless Charlotte was hurt.

Then it was *all* of their business.

"Maddox," Finn growled.

Maddox leaned forward and kissed his daughter's cheek. "Your mother and I will call you tonight."

"Love you, Dad."

"Love you too, baby."

With that, Maddox and Drake left, the tension in the room lowering but not as much as it should have.

Finn met Bram's eyes. The other wolf couldn't keep his gaze for long considering he wasn't as dominant, but he tried enough so as not to challenge but to still hold his stance.

"I'll talk to you later, Charlotte," Bram said finally.

"I don't know that we have much to talk about," Charlotte said firmly.

Bram raised a brow. "Keep thinking that, honey."

Finn blinked. Interesting.

Bram turned on his heel and left. Finn took a deep breath and didn't scent Maddox or Drake nearby. That was good, at least.

Charlotte closed the door firmly behind Bram's retreating back but didn't turn toward Finn.

"Want to tell me what that was about?" Finn asked smoothly.

"Want to tell me what's going on with you and Brynn?" she asked pointedly.

Finn snorted. "Fair enough."

She turned then, playing with her ponytail. "You're okay? I heard about the so-called accident, but everyone said you were fine."

Finn held out his arms. "Just a few twinges that should be gone in a couple of days, if not tomorrow."

She tucked herself close to his body, inhaling deeply before relaxing. She was his family, one of his anchors. He hugged her close, needing the touch as much as she did.

"Don't die on me, Finn. I don't know if I could bear it."

He kissed the top of her head. "I won't," he whispered. "I'm too stubborn."

She sniffed, kissed his chest, then pulled back. "See that you don't. Now, I'm going to go take a hot bath. When and if you're ready to talk about Brynn, you can always come to me."

Finn met his cousin's gaze. "Same goes with Bram."

She nodded then made her way to her part of the house. Finn relaxed as soon as she was gone, knowing he wouldn't be able to hide for too much longer. He'd fucked things up with Brynn by kissing her. Now he couldn't get enough of her, and he didn't know what that meant. He'd have to figure it out though because he had to see her again. There was no getting out of it—no choosing other partners. He and Brynn were too visible, too connected.

He just hoped he hadn't lost everything with one moment of passion. Because he wasn't sure what he'd do if that were the case. He'd had a taste of Brynn and wanted more.

He only hoped she'd be able to give it.

****

The scream woke her.

Brynn shot up from bed, clutching the sheet to her chest as she tried to calm her racing heart. Her throat ached, and she knew the scream had come from her.

The screams always came from her.

She wiped her palm on the bed, her skin clammy, then let the sheet fall to her waist so she could wipe her other palm. The coolness of the room brushed along her skin and bare breasts but didn't help the beat of her heart.

She'd dreamt about her father. About the torture he'd put her through. He'd always liked to watch her bleed, to hear her scream. She might have stopped crying at a young age because she couldn't give him the satisfaction, but sometimes, she couldn't hold back the screams.

She swallowed the bile that had risen to her throat and pulled the sheet fully off her body. She always slept naked. She loved the feel of silk or cotton on her skin as she slept. Her past lovers had enjoyed it, as well. Though now she could only think of Finn sleeping next to her, naked, and even appreciating her form.

She shook, this time for a different reason than the dream. She could still remember the feel of his body pressed close to hers, the feel of the hard line of his cock against her belly.

And...enough of that.

The sun had just started to rise over the ridge so it wasn't too early for her to be up and about. Finn would be showing up later that day for a debriefing. As it was also a new moon, he'd discussed going on a run with Gideon and Brie with the rest of Brynn's brothers going along just because they could. Shifters didn't *need* to shift with the phases of the moon, but they liked to. During a full moon, she could feel the pull on her wolf and her skin always felt more sensitive. Back before she'd caught sight of Finn for the first time, she'd pair off with a single male wolf to ride out the rest of the moon and relieve some tension. Now she rode the tension on her own, never able to fully relax.

It didn't matter, though. Not now. Instead of dwelling like she'd been prone to do lately, she took a quick shower and dressed for the day in tight cargo pants and a couple of tanks. She had to do a few runs as a human, and wasn't in the mood to dress up for Finn—not that she ever truly dressed up for him to begin with.

Her bones tired from her lack of deep sleep, she stretched as she made her way out of her home and to the center of the den. She wanted to talk to Ryder and steal some of his coffee. Like the Redwoods, the Talons had a community area with shops, schools, and everything a wolf might need in case they never wanted to leave the den wards. The Talons were a little more localized in terms of their homes, however. Some still lived in barracks, and others lived in duplexes rather than single-family homes. All of her family lived interspersed within the den population rather than set apart. The Jamensons had their own section since their family was so large and was growing by the generation. It made sense with them since they could feel safe and have privacy. The Brentwoods were a different matter. When Gideon became Alpha, they were essentially starting from scratch with dark scars jaggedly cut across the population. So the Brentwoods lived all over the den. They weren't as close as the Jamensons—their past, paved with blood, not allowing that—but they were getting close.

Finally.

"Brynn."

She stopped where she was, closing her eyes at the voice behind her. She didn't slump or let out a breath. Katherine would take that as a sign of weakness—not an indicator that Brynn with this close to kicking the other woman's ass.

Brynn slowly turned on her heel. "Yes? Is there something I can do for you?"

Katherine met her gaze and didn't back down.

A clear challenge.

Fuck. And Brynn hadn't even had coffee yet. She was so not in the mood for this.

The other woman kept staring, though the strain around her eyes told Brynn the other woman would back down eventually. Or do something stupid like try to claw at her. Though Katherine desperately wanted to be Alpha female, she just wasn't dominant enough.

It wasn't Brynn's fault that she'd been born with that type of strength. It also wasn't her fault that she didn't have a clear place in the Pack hierarchy. But she could only blame the moon goddess for so long before she became as worthless as the wolf in front of her.

"I'm not in the mood to deal with this right now, Katherine," Brynn said slowly, her tone deceptively dull. "You tried this recently and you ended up in the dirt. What do you hope to gain by this?"

"You're where you are because of your brother and yet you don't deserve it," Katherine spat out. "You do nothing for this Pack. You just prance around with that Redwood prince like you're something special to him. I don't scent him on you so you can't even get a wolf from another Pack to rut with you. You're *nothing*."

That barb hurt more than it should have. Everything Katherine said was true in a way, but Brynn was smarter than that. At least with coffee and sleep she was.

Brynn let out a low growl. A warning.

"Katherine," Iona, another dominant wolf said from the side. "Let it go." Iona was more dominant that Katherine, but ranked lower because she'd fucked up with Gideon during his mating with Brie. Iona wasn't a threat anymore, but Brynn didn't like the other woman interfering.

"Go home, Iona," Katherine bit out. "This isn't your concern."

"Enough," Brynn growled.

"No," Katherine snarled.

Brynn jumped. Before the other woman knew what was happening, Brynn had Katherine face down in the dirt, her arms bent back at an awkward angle. Katherine let out a whimper, and Brynn's wolf preened.

"Go the fuck home, Katherine." Brynn didn't even sound out of breath. She was *that* dominant. "I'm done with you." She pushed Katherine down into the dirt before letting her go and walking away. She gave her back to the other wolf, a clear sign that she didn't think Katherine was worth looking out for. Oh, she could move faster than the other woman and kept her senses out in case the bitch tried something, but she was *done*.

This was just one more challenge to add to the countless she'd faced since her father had died. She'd gone from one form of torture to the next.

"Brynn."

She closed her eyes. *Of course.*

Of course, Finn would be here to see her challenge, to see part of her shame.

"What do you want, Finn? You're here early."

She looked over her shoulder as he jogged toward her. Iona had dragged Katherine away, and Brynn was glad of it.

"I couldn't sleep."

That made two of them.

"What do you want?" she asked again.

"I came to see if you wanted breakfast. But first, are you okay?"

She snarled at him. "I'm fine. I'm not going to faint and cry because some wolf thinks she's better than me. I'm not where I am because I can't take a few challenges."

He held up his hands in a position of surrender. "I was just asking because challenges suck. I deal with them, too."

She raised her brows.

"I might be Heir, but I also have to prove to the Pack that I'm strong. Just because I hold the title doesn't mean I'm dominant. Sure, that's the case most times, but the Pack needs to see it, too."

She relaxed marginally. "I forget that. I guess the others have to deal with their own forms of challenges." She shrugged. "I think I just have to deal with a few more than them."

He nodded, his gaze studying her face. "I can see that as you don't have a set title but have the strength to have any of them. I don't know what the moon goddess was thinking when it came to you."

That was the understatement of the century.

Something he said came back to her. "Wait. You came here to ask me to breakfast? We have phones you know. Plus, I thought we were done with the whole in public thing together."

Finn raised a brow. It was wrong that she still found that sexy. "I could have called, but I needed the fresh air. And you know as well as I do that we're too public to change things now. You're stuck with me, Brynn. Like it or not."

That wasn't the problem. She liked it. A little too much.

So she said the only thing she could say. "Fine."

CHAPTER EIGHT

Fine was a better answer than Finn could have hoped for, in all honestly. At least she hadn't clawed his face for showing up. He hadn't been able to sleep, that much was true. But it was because he kept thinking of Brynn beneath him. And then that wasn't good enough because he wanted her on top of him, taking over, showing him that she could ride him just has hard as he could ride her.

Hence the lack of sleep.

Brynn had agreed to breakfast, and that had to be a step in the right direction. Whatever that direction was, he didn't know, but at least she wasn't looking at him like she wanted to kill him.

She sat across from him outside of the morning café, her hands wrapped around her coffee cup. She hadn't said much to him, but since they were in public, she hadn't snarled or snapped at him either.

"Need a refill?" he asked, nodding toward her cup. She looked up at him, her eyes shifting back and forth across their surroundings.

Things had been tense since they'd gotten there—even more so than usual. It wasn't even about them at that point, though he knew that problem was still there, lurking under the surface, ready to burst out at any moment and threaten them both. Yet through all of that, it was the feeling of something coming, something he couldn't quite put his finger on that had him sitting a little stiffer than usual.

"I'm okay. Thanks." She let out a breath. "Something's weird. Isn't it?"

He snorted, and she rolled her eyes. Damn, he didn't think she could do something as simple as that—not around him. He liked it. Liked knowing she had something other than a snarl for him.

"I meant sitting right here, together, out in the open. The news had the accident on their broadcast, so even though we're not in a small town, people have probably recognized us at this point. But, it's not even that..."

He frowned. "I know what you mean. There's something in the air, something coming."

She shivered, and he held back the need to do the same. "I don't like this feeling."

"I'm with you there."

She let out a breath then stood up, setting her coffee cup down on the table. "I need to use the restroom. Keep an eye out because I know we're not safe. And if both of us are on edge because we have a feeling about something? I'd rather be careful that not."

He nodded, running a hand along his chin. He needed a shave but had been too out of it to deal with grooming that morning. "Be alert. Someone tried to come at us yesterday." He could still hear the mother's scream, and wasn't sure he'd be getting that out of his head any time soon.

She met his gaze, an emotion he couldn't place flashing over her eyes in a bare instant. "I know." Her voice lowered. "I remember, Finn. I remember what you did to save that little girl yesterday. And I'm pretty sure the humans looking as us right now remember, as well. That's not something you forget." She rolled her shoulders back. "Try not to get hit by a car while I'm gone."

He raised a brow at her tone. "I'll do my best," he said dryly.

He watched her walk away because how could he not? She filled out a pair of jeans nicely, the denim clinging to her curves much like he wanted to. He might be on alert and his senses on their surroundings, but he was still a man, still a wolf.

He wanted Brynn Brentwood, and still had no idea what to do about it.

A little girl looked at him from the table across the way, her eyes wide. Her father tugged on her pigtail, his eyes glaring at Finn, and the little girl turned her attention back to her meal.

At least they didn't get up and walk away because they realized they were eating next to wolves. That had to be some progress.

But it wasn't enough. They were only a small cog in the process of what it would take to be free and out in the open.

His phone buzzed and he pulled it out, answering when he saw his cousin Parker's name light up on the screen. Parker was North and Lexi's son, though not a Jamenson by birth as he'd been adopted in years ago. His older cousin was the Voice of the Redwoods, the wolf that could easily move from Pack to Pack and try to broker treaties. When the former Talon Alpha had shown the world that the wolves existed, it wasn't merely the Talons or the Redwoods that had been shoved out into the open. The entire world had been cracked to the point that long-held secrets were just now slithering out.

The government had known about many of the Packs before the Unveiling. There was no way around that, not in the technological age they lived in. But the right people had known for a time, and wolves had been secretly in some power positions. Those wolves were still hidden from the humans, their other halves buried deep.

But not everyone had a choice when it came to being out in public with what they truly were.

And Parker's job for over a decade now had been to work with the Redwood and Talon council and go to other Packs in person to ensure that every wolf was on the same page. It was an impossible task with so many dominant wolves and personalities, but Parker had a way about him that made it somewhat work.

Treaties and plans for the future could be done by phone and screen, but with many of the Alpha wolves far older than the world they lived in, face to face meetings were the only way to accomplish that. Parker had a duty to his Pack and to all the Packs, and Finn thought his cousin was damn good at it.

"Parker," he said when he answered, his attention mostly on his surroundings. His wolf was at the surface, on edge, but it was nothing new these days.

"Hey, Finn," Parker said, his deep voice holding a hint of a laugh. Parker had been through shit during the early years of his life, but he always held a smile and a laugh for those close to him.

"What are you up to? Calling just to shoot the shit?" He hoped so. He hoped that Parker's duty was on the right path and he had the time to just talk to his family. Because Finn honestly didn't want to deal with any new issues right then. He had enough on his plate with the Pack, the humans, and, of course,

Brynn. That didn't mean he wouldn't drop everything to help Parker. Because he would. The man was family, maybe not blood, but family.

"I'm just checking in," Parker answered. "It's been awhile since I've called, and I wanted to know how things were going. Brynn slice your balls off yet?"

Finn didn't want to think about Brynn and his balls, not when he had to act normal and still talk with Parker. His wolf remained silent through it all, making Finn want to scream. Why couldn't his wolf want her? Why couldn't his wolf act like a normal shifter and push him when it mattered?

"My balls are just fine, thanks for your concern," he said dryly. He put thoughts of his wolf and what it wouldn't do out of his mind.

"Good to know." Parker sighed. "I heard about the car coming after you. I'm glad you saved the girl, by the way. Jesus, what are these humans thinking? They almost killed one of their own in their blind hatred of us."

"You said it yourself right then, Park. They aren't thinking. They're blind when it comes to anything other than their purpose. What that purpose exactly is? I don't know. Were they coming after Brynn and me because of who we are in terms of being shifters? Was it random that they found us? Or is it because Brynn and I are out in public more than others, and it would have been a better symbol to hurt us?" He held back a growl at the thought of Brynn being hurt. She might be fucking strong as hell and fully capable of handling herself, but damn it, he couldn't see her hurt.

Parker growled, as well. "I don't fucking know, and that's what makes this so dangerous. We don't know what the next step is. And I'm afraid we won't know until something serious happens and people get hurt."

That was what Finn was afraid of, as well. Because they didn't know what the others were thinking. It didn't matter that they'd done their best to protect their dens from the inevitable fallout. It didn't matter that they'd put people in key positions for the worst.

They couldn't get into the minds of the humans who hated them—or were merely uncertain of them. Their lives rested on the morals of a set of humans he couldn't understand, and that didn't sit well on his shoulders. The wolf in him wanted to howl, wanted to protect all in his care. Finn relished that, however, because it meant his wolf was actually listening.

That had to be something these days.

"I hate that most of us are hiding," Parker mumbled.

"Is it bad out there?" Finn asked. He honestly didn't know much about the other Packs. Most shifters were secretive for a reason.

"It's not great," Parker hedged. His cousin knew when to keep things close to the vest, especially since it was never safe for a wolf to be out in the open as he was within so many other Packs. "Listen, I have to go. I only wanted to call and make sure you were okay, really. I'll come home soon to check in. Mom and Dad miss me."

Finn grinned at that. "We all do, cousin. Be safe."

"I will. And watch your back, Finn. I don't have a good feeling."

Finn sat up straighter at the echo of his earlier conversation with Brynn. There was something on the wind, something the moon goddess wanted to tell them. The moon goddess didn't speak directly to most of them. In fact, Finn only knew of his aunt Lexi, Parker's mother, and Lexi's brother Logan who had heard the moon goddess in his lifetime. However, though the moon goddess didn't speak to them directly, they still got feelings over time. With so many of them feeling it, Finn knew it wasn't just happenstance.

Something was coming.

Only Finn was afraid they wouldn't know what it was until it was too late.

He spoke to Parker for a few more minutes before hanging up. As soon as he did, Brynn walked toward the table and sat down. He raised a brow. "Were you waiting for me to finish my call?"

She shrugged, her attention on their surroundings. "I could hear most of it since, hello, wolf, but I tried to give you some semblance of privacy."

He ran a hand over his face. "Thanks. Parker is making inroads, or at least I think so. He doesn't talk about it much."

Brynn met his gaze, a frown on her face. "I don't know much about what he does because he's not Pack. But I know he's doing it for *all* Packs, not only the Redwoods. For that, I will help him whenever he needs it."

Pride filled him at Brynn's words. She was just so fucking strong—and smart. And loyal. And just a phenomenal wolf.

Not that he could tell her that.

Brynn frowned over his shoulder and he turned to see what she was looking at. "Isn't that Franklin? And, Seth. Right? He's one of yours if I recall."

Finn narrowed his eyes at the two wolves walking down the street talking and laughing as if they hadn't a care in the world. It did his heart good to see it. Two wolves from different Packs, looking like they were actually enjoying themselves. And from the subtle touches, he had a feeling they were well into their own courting and mating dance. "Yeah, he's one of mine. Franklin's yours, right?"

"Yeah," she answered, her voice tense. "I didn't know they'd be outside the den today."

He looked back at Brynn. "They aren't locked inside, Brynn. They need some semblance of freedom wherever they can take it."

She let out an audible breath. "I know, but—" She was up out of her chair before she'd finished her sentence, and Finn was right on her tail. He didn't see what she had, but he followed, trusting her instincts implicitly.

A car sped toward Franklin and Seth, its window sliding down as it neared the two. The glint of sun on metal caught his eye and he growled. Finn lowered his head and put his wolf into his speed, trying to catch up to the two men before something bad happened.

"Franklin! Seth! Down!" Brynn called as she ran.

But it was too late.

The two wolves tried to move out of the way, but the bullets sprayed, hitting them over and over until they fell to their knees, blood pooling around their bodies. The car sped off, the screech of tires echoing in Finn's ears. He howled as he went to follow the car, trying to look at who was in it, but it sped away, far too fast for him.

His wolf wanted to follow anyway. It needed blood. Needed vengeance.

"Finn! I need you."

He froze at Brynn's shaky words.

I need you.

Finn ran back to her, aware of people screaming, calling for ambulances, scared out of their minds.

Brynn knelt between the two men, her eyes wolf, her shoulders tense. She had one hand over Franklin's chest, the other on Seth's abdomen. "I need you, Finn."

He knelt in front of her. "I'm here. What do you need me to do?"

She met his gaze, her jaw tight. "Help your wolf, I'll help mine. Your bonds to him should keep him alive." Her voice broke, but she did not cry. So fucking strong. "I don't have the same bonds as you, but I'll do my best." Both men were unconscious, their hands reaching out to one another as if they'd fallen and tried for each other, only to come up short.

His heart broke, but he couldn't think about that. Not yet. Not when his wolf and one of Brynn's wolves lay dying on a street corner because people didn't understand the love of two men, two wolves, two people so unlike the true monsters who'd done this.

He nodded quickly, pulling out his phone to call his Alpha even as he placed his hand over Brynn's. She shook under his touch before removing her blood-slicked hand from his and moving it to her fallen Pack member. He put the phone on his shoulder as it connected to his father, keeping both hands on Seth's wounds.

He wasn't a Healer, but damn it, this didn't look good. Wolves could heal quickly and get up after a lot of injuries, but so many bullets in a short time was stretching it, even for a wolf as strong as Finn.

Seth and Franklin weren't as strong as him.

"Finn." His Alpha's voice soothed Finn's wolf slightly. "I felt the pain along the bonds. I'm sending out Hannah, Mark, and Josh. Don't let the humans take them to their hospital. Our people are two minutes out from you. Keep them alive, Finn. Use the bonds."

"And the Talons?" he gritted out, pushing his power toward Seth. The heat from his wolf shoved down the bond and into Seth's heart. The fallen Redwood sucked in a breath and Finn wanted to shout. Thank the goddess. "Brynn doesn't have the same bonds."

Kade cursed. "Jasper is calling Walker to our den now. It's faster to get everyone here and out of the way of human eyes. Do your best to keep that wolf alive. You hear me? You might not be his Heir, but you're fucking strong. Keep our people alive, Finn."

Finn let the phone fall to the pavement when Kade ended the call. "Brynn?"

"I heard," she gritted out. "I'll do what I can. But Finn?"

"I know." He growled low and the humans that had come closer backed away slowly. So much for looking innocent and calm. But there was only so much he could take before the dam broke and the need to protect what was his overtook everything else.

Another vehicle stopped in front of them, the tires screeching again. Finn looked up, growling, ready to kill anyone who dared come at him. He scented Hannah and Josh as they jumped out of the van and he relaxed somewhat. Mark followed them, his younger brother and new Healer holding his chin high.

"Get them in the van," Josh barked out. He wasn't a wolf, but mated into the Pack, yet Finn listened to the order and didn't hesitate.

Finn picked up Seth, cradling him close. Thankfully, the man was out cold because moving him like this was going to hurt like hell. But they didn't have a choice when it came to the health and safety of what was theirs. It would look odd to humans, but they'd deal with that later. Hannah had her arms out, Healing as she walked beside Finn. She murmured under her breath, her hands shaking as she did.

Mark went to Brynn's side as she lifted Franklin. It looked awkward, but she had a wolf's strength. Finn lifted Seth into the back of the van and stepped in behind him and Hannah.

Mark got in with Franklin, his eyes narrowed. "I can't Heal him directly but I can do some. Plus, North and Noah trained me." That meant Mark not only could use his connection to the moon goddess to help, but he was also a medic. Brynn seemed to understand that Franklin would be in the best hands possible and stepped back.

"I'll ride up front with Josh and call my contacts." She met Finn's gaze. "This isn't over."

He shook his head, and she slammed the van doors.

It wasn't over by a long shot. But with the blood of his Pack on his hands, he didn't know what they'd do next.

Blood has been spilled.

He prayed a true war hadn't begun.

****

Brynn washed the blood off her hands, knowing she'd forever remember the scent of Franklin's blood on her skin. The fact that it had been mixed with Seth's only made the pain worse.

Franklin had died because she wasn't strong enough.

She wasn't bonded to the Pack like those who were true powers were. If she'd been almost anyone else in her family, Franklin would have stood a chance. But she wasn't. Franklin had died with her hands on his heart, doing her best to use her wolf to save him.

But it hadn't worked.

She'd been too far from her den, too far from her Healer to save him.

Mark and Hannah had done their best to save Franklin, but her wolf had died before they'd even made it to the Redwood den where Walker had rushed to meet them.

Her wolf had died, and there was nothing she could have done.

Nothing.

Seth would live only because Finn had used most of his energy to push life into Seth's body. Without Finn, Seth would have died, as well.

There were only so many bullets a body could take before it gave out.

No one blamed her for what had happened, but she couldn't help but blame herself. Seth would wake knowing the man he'd been on his way to mating would never wake with him. Seth would never have a future with the man he'd fallen in love with. The two had apparently been waiting to seal the bond until after they'd talked to the two Alphas. They had wanted permission, though they never would have needed it. They would have been one of the many new inter-Pack matings that would have strengthened the bonds between the Packs. Perhaps if they had been bonded, they would have been able to use each other to live. Perhaps if they had been bonded, Finn could have saved them both.

But no one would know if that would have happened.

A future as bright as theirs would never come to be because someone had run them down with a spray of bullets, wiping out their potential bond and existence before it even stood a chance.

She braced herself against her bathroom sink, knowing she needed to suck it up. She couldn't be who she was and look like she wanted to sob in a corner because of the unfairness of it all.

She and Finn had lived. Yet Franklin had not. And Seth would take months to fully heal.

Brynn met her gaze in the bathroom mirror, annoyed that her wolf was still so close to the surface. She'd need a run soon because there was no way she'd be able to keep in control at this rate. Her wolf wanted blood, and yet it couldn't have it. Not with so many uncertainties.

She let out a breath and moved back into her living room, not surprised to see Ryder there, sitting on the couch with his forearms resting on his legs. Her brother was the quiet one of the group. All of her family had been through hell, and Ryder had his own past to deal with. Because of that, he would sit down and listen to anything she had to say without judgment. He was such a good brother that way.

And she honestly didn't want to talk to him right then.

"Brynn," he said softly. "It wasn't your fault."

Damn the man and knowing exactly what to say. He wasn't even the Omega, and yet he knew the heart of the matter. Brandon, the true Omega and one of the Brentwood triplets, was even better at it, but he did his best not to look too hard at her emotions. He loved her enough to know that one wrong tug on the bond and she'd break.

Brandon had to know she was dying inside.

And from the look on Ryder's face, he knew, as well.

She didn't answer him. She knew it wasn't her fault logically, but since when did wolves use pure logic?

"I know you're hurting from Franklin, but Brynn, it's more than that. You've been hurting for over a year."

She looked away, not wanting to face him but knowing she couldn't hide anymore. "We all have reasons for our pain," she hedged.

Ryder growled softly. "Don't cop out. Do you think I can stand by and watch my only sister hide away from herself because of a new pain? It's not the same as it was before. If you were merely healing from what Dad did to us all those years ago, then I'd stand back because we all needed time after that. We still need that time. If your strain on the bonds between us were due to the unrest in our world, then I'd stand by your side and fight whatever enemy we faced. But this is different, and we both know it." He reached out and gripped her hand, surprising her. The Brentwoods hugged and touched one another when needed because, after all, they were wolves. But Ryder didn't go out of his way to be affectionate. He had his reasons—ones she didn't press because, as he'd said, they had a right to their own way of healing.

"Brynn."

She met his gaze, her heart in her throat. "Finn is my mate," she blurted.

Ryder's eyes widened, his jaw going slack. "What the fuck?" he rasped.

Tears filled her eyes, surprising her. She didn't cry. She *couldn't*. Ryder looked at her and moved to her side, pulling her into his arms quickly. She rested her head on his shoulder, her body trembling.

"Tell me what happened so I don't kill him," he whispered. "Or maybe I'll kill him anyway. Fuck the treaty."

Her quiet and soft-spoken Ryder.

"I knew the first time I saw his face full-on." She sucked in a breath. "I mean, I'd seen him in the distance when he was younger, and even saw him a bit more a few years ago. But it wasn't until Gideon and Brie's mating ceremony that I knew in truth. Finn was mine. My wolf wanted him, pushed me so hard I almost shifted right then." She wiped her face, annoyed she'd let the tears fall in the first place.

"And he just walked away?" Ryder asked. He didn't yell, didn't growl or move so quickly that she startled. Instead, he sat there and let her speak.

She told him everything that had happened since the mating ceremony when she'd looked at Finn's face and *knew* he didn't know, that the moon goddess had made a mistake with her.

She was nothing but a mistake.

Ryder held her closer as she finished, even telling him about the alley and Finn's words. She blushed during it, but she didn't care. It felt *good* to tell him about it all. She would have told Brie since the other woman was her only female friend these days with all of the dominance challenges, but this was the one thing she couldn't go to her for. Not when Brie and Finn were so close.

"Oh, Brynn."

She snorted, her sinuses pulsing after her hard cry. "I know."

"What are you going to do, baby girl?"

She smiled at his words, despite the agony in her heart. She wasn't a little girl, nor a baby anymore, but Ryder was her older brother, and some things would never change.

"I don't know. I hate that I'm sitting here crying and worrying about myself when our Pack is hurting. Seth will wake up soon, if he hasn't already, and know he doesn't have the future he thought he would. How selfish am I that I can't just get over this?"

"You're not supposed to get over it. And I think you're breaking harder now *because* of what happened this morning. You're allowed to feel more than one thing. You're allowed to be hurting because of something that has been grating on you for far too long. I don't think worse of you for it, and you can be damn sure none of the others will."

She didn't say anything, her mind still working through everything that had happened even in the last week.

"I know this isn't what you want to hear, but Brynn, you need to tell him."

She shook her head. "I can't. If I do, I'll be weak. He'll know that weakness, and I can't allow that to happen."

He sighed. "You will never be weak, no matter what you think. Your wolf needs this, as do you. And Finn needs it too, baby girl. He needs to know what he's missing. If you don't tell him, then I might be forced to kick his ass because I'm so fucking pissed that he's hurting you by not knowing, Brynn. There has to be a reason, and hiding from it isn't helping anyone."

She licked her lips. "What happens when I tell him? What then? *Both* of us will know that we're missing something."

"Or maybe you can find a way. Never discount the moon goddess."

Brynn had been discounted her entire existence thanks to the moon goddess and her grand plans. It would take more than a nudge from her brother for

Brynn to bare her belly and the truth. She'd spent far too long proving that she could handle anything. She wasn't sure she was ready—if she could ever *be* ready for Finn to knowingly turn her away.

For if he did that, she'd shatter in truth.

And there was no coming back from that.

PERSUASION

T he delicate balance between peace and war was not something to be cared for lightly. When one wanted to gently align key elements so said balance would shift at the precise moment, then nothing else could matter.

Senator Charles McMaster knew better than anyone that the art of war wasn't fought in one evening. Instead, it took years to put the key pieces in place. With the aid of General Keith Montag, the plan would fall into place soon.

It was all about persuasion.

Persuading the right humans to fall in line.

Persuading the right shifter-haters to act when required.

Persuading the right doctors to follow him into the abyss of shifter research.

Charles adjusted the knot of his tie so it lay perfectly over his chest. It wouldn't do to look anything but perfect. The world needed to see a caring and compassionate activist in one frame, and one who would stand up for their rights in the other.

Wolves could never be allowed to know who truly controlled their future.

Because one day, they would feel the true agony of their existence.

"Are you ready to see the subject?" Montag asked, his voice almost a growl. The man was so uncouth, almost like the wolves they hunted. But Charles needed Montag for his plan to work.

Charles turned toward the General and raised a brow. "Of course. Has there been any progress since the last phase of the moon?"

Montag shook his head. "No. The damn beast won't shift. But we'll get him to. If not, then he'll end up with the others, and we'll find a new subject." Montag shrugged. "It's not like we don't know where the others are."

Charles nodded slightly. "True, of course." They'd known for far longer than the wolves were aware, but then again, Charles did his best to be one step ahead of the game.

He followed Montag toward the lower basement where the beginning of their journey had occurred and where many of the next stages would remain. Cages lined the walls while a door at the other end of the long room led the way to the more...daunting prospects.

This was only phase one, of course. Charles needed the humans to remain fearful of what they didn't know. The wolves were playing nice so far and being oh so careful. That wouldn't remain the case for long so Charles would do what he could to ensure that he used this pause in their hostility to his and Montag's advantage.

He would soon...persuade the next set of humans to fight in his war. Only they wouldn't know they were doing it until it was too late.

Charles stared dispassionately at the wolf in human form, who huddled naked in the cage. If it didn't shift soon, it would die. Maybe not by genetics, but by those Charles employed. It wouldn't do for him to do it himself. He didn't do the dirty work. That's why he had Montag.

The General kept the cage shut but stuck a cattle prod through the bars. The beast screamed, but again, didn't shift.

What a waste.

No matter, however. Soon, the next step in his plan would take place, and the humans would remain fearful of the wolves they didn't know. It was unfortunate that the Heir had saved that small child. It was even more unfortunate that it looked as if the Heir and the Talon woman had done their best to save the two wolves who Charles had been keeping an eye on. The humans were seeing those two act with valor far too many times for Charles' liking.

He needed the masses to fear the wolves, not pause to think of those two's actions.

It seemed he needed to add one more piece to the plan.

A little prodding, a little persuasion, and the extremists who had been unknowingly aiding him would keep up their work.

The beast screamed again, and this time, Charles let one side of his mouth lift up in a grin.

The delicate balance would be his to play with, his to manipulate. It was what he'd been born for. It was what others would bleed for.

CHAPTER NINE

F inn ran a hand over his mouth, nodding at the sentries at the Talon gate. He slid though the wards, ignoring the pinpricks of sensation dancing along his skin. When he went through the Redwood wards, it was as if he were coming home, the magic welcoming him. This was more like something agreeing to let him stay, but not for long. The magic knew he wasn't a Talon and wanted Finn to know that, as well.

The wards provided the last set of protections for their people, so he wouldn't begrudge it. If they didn't have them, then there would be no barrier between them and the humans. And until the wolves knew *exactly* what the humans were going to do, then the wards would be needed. The magic kept humans out; not animals or weather. It even let trees grow and seed on either side. It only kept those that would—or could—harm them away.

Brandon, Mitchell, and Kameron stood near the entrance, each of them glaring at Finn. Nothing new considering the three of them weren't too keen on their family member spending so much time with a rival male wolf. Brandon and Kameron were two of the triplets but were easy to tell apart considering one was the Omega while the other the Enforcer. Brandon exuded a sense of calm about him because that was his duty and the way of his wolf. Kameron was the Enforcer and looked the part. The Enforcer's job was to protect the Pack from outside forces. They were stronger than most wolves and could sense danger from outside the den walls. Their bonds to the Pack were a form of warning beacon that allowed Kameron to do what he could to save his Pack from a battle *before* it happened. Finn wasn't sure he'd ever seen the man smile. In fact, he wasn't even sure he'd seen an emotion at all from the man. He was ice, harsh and cold but damn good at his job. Such a contrast to his emotional Omega triplet. As Brandon needed to taste every single emotion in the Pack, it made sense that though the two looked alike with their dark hair, dark eyes, and strong jaws, they didn't act alike. Walker, the other triplet who was somewhere else in the den at the moment, was the Healer and fell somewhere in the middle of the two when it came to ice versus warmth.

Mitchell was just an asshole.

The Beta of the Pack was the Brentwood cousin and Max's brother. Finn loved Max. Everything Max did, he did with a smile. He was sweet and loved taking care of those he considered his own. Finn had no idea how Mitchell was able to care for the day-to-day needs of the Pack when he didn't smile, only sneered. Of course, the man could just do that for Finn because, like he'd said, Mitchell was an asshole.

It probably didn't help matters that Finn thought *Brynn* should have been Beta once the moon goddess chose the next generation after the previous Alpha and powers had been killed. Brynn knew her Pack inside and out and put her whole body and soul into their needs and protection. Yet she'd been shunned from the bonds that could have helped her Pack so much more. The fact that the Beta position had gone to a *cousin* rather than Gideon's immediate family was just another slap in the face. Finn knew Brynn loved her entire family, but it had to hurt to see that she couldn't have the same bonds most of them did.

He held back a curse as he remembered the look on her face when they'd lost Franklin. She'd blamed herself, even though he'd tried to tell her it wasn't her fault. She wouldn't listen to him or Walker. She'd gone into herself and walked away before he could do anything to help her.

He wasn't sure what he would have done if she'd have given him a chance, but he would have done *something*. He couldn't stand to watch her in pain and not try to soothe her aches.

"Is there a reason you're here, Jamenson?" Mitchell asked, his brow raised.

Kameron glared.

Brandon studied his face.

Finn didn't lower his gaze. His wolf was stronger than all three of theirs. Maybe not combined in a fight, but in terms of dominance, Finn won.

"I'm here to see Brynn. Thanks for the welcoming committee."

"You've got a mouth on you, pup," Mitchell growled.

Finn raised a brow. "True. I come by it naturally. Now are you going to let me pass? Or are we going to have an issue?" Others had started to gather around them, uncertainty and pain coming off them in waves. Damn it. They'd just lost a Packmate and needed someone to blame. He didn't want to fight, but he also knew these people needed to heal. Finn let his shoulders drop.

"I wanted to make sure she was okay after what happened," Finn said softly. "Plus, we need to talk about the next phase of our plan."

"And you couldn't do that by phone?" Brandon asked, not unkindly. It was as if the wolf were trying to put his finger on something but couldn't quite get it. Finn didn't understand either.

Finn shook his head. "Some things need to be done in person."

Kameron narrowed his eyes but stepped to the side. "Be careful, Finn. She's in pain."

Shock slid through Finn. Kameron wasn't the emotional one, far from it, yet the astute statement surprised him. It seemed Finn needed to keep an open mind when it came to these Brentwoods.

"I don't want to cause any more," he said as he walked past the three. He knew he'd caused a fair share of his own when it came to her, but he hadn't meant to. They just grated on one another, and with the sexual attraction simmering between the two of them, things were bound to explode.

By the time he made it to her place, others had checked him out but hadn't come up to him. It made sense as he wasn't a Talon, but his wolf didn't like the challenges each one presented. This wasn't his Pack, and he couldn't stare down the other wolves and expect submission like he could with the Redwoods. Though he didn't tend to do that anyway with his own Pack, considering they had a symbiotic relationship.

As he lifted his hand to knock, the door opened and Ryder stepped out. Finn moved back and let the other Heir move farther onto the porch.

"Finn," Ryder said with a growl.

That was surprising. Ryder never growled at him. The two of them held the same positions in the Packs and held a mutual respect for one another. What had happened since their last meeting?

Finn tilted his head and studied Ryder's face and saw a knowing in his gaze.

Well, fuck, what had Brynn told him?

"Ryder, go home," Brynn said softly from the doorway. "I can handle this myself."

"Watch yourself, wolf," Ryder snapped then loped away, leaving Finn confused as hell.

"What the hell just happened?" he asked as he turned toward Brynn. She had her hair down so it brushed the tops of her breasts. She wore a pair of tiny shorts and a tank with no bra. Her nipples pebbled against the fabric under his gaze, and he had to swallow hard so he could keep breathing.

"Are you going to come in? Or are you going to stare at my breasts for the rest of the evening?"

He pulled his gaze from her chest, though he would have liked to stare for the rest of the evening. That wasn't why he'd come over though.

She didn't move out of the way, instead, she just stared at him.

"Are you going to let me in?" he asked, knowing there was a possibility she'd say no. She'd already invited him in, but she hadn't moved.

She finally moved to the side and he walked in, brushing along her skin as he did so. They both sucked in a breath at the contact. He was so on edge that he could barely think. He had to remind himself that wasn't why he'd come to her place. This wasn't about him, but about her.

It had to be.

"I'd ask how you're doing, but now that I think about it, it's a fucking useless question." He ran a hand through his hair and turned to look at her. She'd closed the front door and stood in front of it, her hands behind her back. Her eyes were so wide that she looked years younger. The gold rim around her eyes though told him that her wolf was far too close to the surface. She'd need a run soon if she wanted to keep sane.

The delicate balance between human and wolf would never cease to be a sense of struggle for their kind. It was how they lived, but it didn't make it easy.

"He died because I'm not connected to the Pack like I should be, Finn. So, no, I'm not doing well or good or anything but completely shitty right now."

Finn took a step forward and she held out her arm. "Brynn, let me help."

She snorted. "How can you help, Finn? Huh? How can you? You're someone that I wasn't supposed to see again. You weren't supposed to be with me at all. We decided that we weren't going to do this anymore. And then we went back on that because it's for the good of our Packs. What good have we done? What good could we have done when my Pack is still dying despite all I'm trying to do for them?"

He stepped closer and she didn't move her arm. He kept going until her hand landed on his chest. The contact sent a shock through both of them, but he didn't move back.

"Brynn. Let me help."

"How?" she asked, her voice cracking. Her eyes widened even more than they already were and she shook her head. "I can't cry in front of you. I can't break down. You bring out the worst in me, and I don't know why." She gave a watery snort. "No, actually I *do* know why, but there's nothing I can do about it, is there?"

He didn't understand her cryptic comment, but hell, he didn't understand most of her moods anyway. All he knew was that she was hurting and her wolf needed to run. That was something he could help with.

Finn reached up and gently ran his fingers along her wrist. Her fingers tightened on his chest, her claws peeking through her fingers and scraping his skin. He didn't flinch as she drew blood. The coppery scent filled the air and Brynn let out a whimper.

She'd been so tightly strung for so long, trying to keep strong for her Pack and having to deal with him when he knew she truly didn't want to, couldn't want to, that she was about to break.

"Run with me."

She shook her head. "I can't, Finn. If I shift now, the wolf will be in control." She sucked in a breath. "I need to be stronger than this."

He reached up with his other hand slowly. She froze but didn't pull away as he cupped her face. "Let me help. You're afraid to show a lack of control in front of your Pack. I get it. I've been there. But I'm not your Pack. You can break down if you need to, shift and let your wolf roam free. I'll be there to make sure you're not going too far. I can't pull you back from your bonds, but I can get to you. You know I already get to you so I'll use that to make sure you come back to your Pack. Let me help you, Brynn. Losing a Pack member should never happen. Not with the way we live, but when it does, we all feel the pain of a thousand losses. Let me help."

Brynn clenched her jaw, her face defiant. He kept his hold on her cheek and let her claws dig deeper into his chest. The pain helped keep his control locked down tight. He wouldn't let her hurt herself because she felt inadequate. The world was crashing down around them, and yet all he could do was focus on the woman in front of him.

He'd think about the implications of that thought later.

Brynn sucked in a breath then lowered her head. "I...I need to run." She said this so low that Finn had trouble hearing her, but he didn't wait long enough for her to change her mind.

Instead, he backed up a step, her claws leaving small gouges along his skin. "Come on, then. Show me where you want to run. I don't know your den." He tilted his head. "I'd offer my den so your Pack won't see you, but that's too far away. Plus, I don't think you'd be as comfortable with so many strangers."

Her gaze was on the blood on his chest, and he wanted to curse.

"You didn't hurt me, Brynn. I liked it. Now, come on."

She shook her head then took a deep breath. "Thank you. I need to get out of my head and then I'll be back."

"I know. Sometimes we need to just let it go. I get it."

With that, he reached behind her and opened the front door. She stepped out of the way and followed him to the porch. He could feel the stares of the dominant wolves on him as he and Brynn made their way to one of the forested areas of the den where Brynn wanted to run.

Brynn let out a curse as soon as they reached the tree line. "I don't think you should come to the den anymore."

He almost tripped over a rock at her words. "Excuse me?" He let the Heir come into his voice, aware that he probably was going to piss her off. Again. "I thought our Packs had a treaty."

Brynn blew a raspberry as they kept moving at a brisk pace. "It's not a Pack versus Pack thing, Finn. Not really. You're just so fucking dominant that the other wolves don't know what to do with themselves. It's one of the reasons Gideon doesn't go to visit Brie's family all the time, and why Kade doesn't stop by for coffee. They're just too dominant to be around a lot of wolves that can't help but want to challenge them since they aren't sure of the ranking of that particular wolf within the Pack. And since it's two different Packs, it becomes an issue. We're the only two Packs I know of that have a treaty such as ours with so many of us going from den to den."

Finn lifted a lip in a snarl. "I know they want to challenge me and can't, but the Alphas don't go to the other dens for safety and as a sign of respect."

"That's part of it, sure, but all dominant wolves need to be aware of how they affect those around them."

"You're talking to me like I'm a pup, Brynn. I know what my presence does. I can't help how they react to me, but I don't fight back. I let them stare and try to challenge. I don't growl or bite. I know I'm on their territory, so I do my best not to let my wolf out. I only come to the den to see you, you know. I don't even come to the Talons to see Brie." He hadn't even realized that was the case until he'd said it.

Strange.

Brynn let out a breath then stopped between a small circle of trees where a fallen log acted as a bench. "I know that. But it's still a lot for them. Especially right now."

Finn shook his head. "Then you'll come to the Redwoods? Because if I can't come here, you'll have to come there."

"Who says I have to meet you inside a den at all? We can call, text, or just meet outside. No matter the plans, we don't need to see each other outside that."

"You know that's not the case. Not anymore." He didn't know what he was saying or why he was saying it, but he knew it was the truth right then.

"I can't deal with this right now. I need to run." Brynn sucked on her lips and shook her head before stripping off her tank top.

Finn looked away before he did something stupid like crush his mouth to hers. Wolves were used to nudity. When they shifted, it wasn't as if their clothes magically fell away. If they didn't strip down before they shifted to wolf, they'd end up tangled in their clothes. Brynn being naked shouldn't bother him. He should have been able to see her take off her clothes in front of him and shift to a wolf and be fine with it. They were wolves. That was how things were done. Wolves didn't let their eyes linger unless they were mates or had privileges that he didn't have with Brynn. They weren't as crass as to get off on another wolf doing what they had to in order to shift.

Yet Finn couldn't hold back the urge to take her. Instead, he pulled his shirt over his head and undid his jeans. He heard her shuck off her shorts and bend down near the log. He wouldn't think about her curves or how fucking sexy she was when they were doing this. He had to be stronger than that. He quickly toed off his shoes and stepped out of his jeans before kneeling down.

"I'll follow you," Finn said. "Once we're wolves, I'll follow where you want to go. If I sense you need me to, I'll pull you back, but just let go, Brynn."

"Thank you," she whispered.

He still didn't look at her, afraid of his own control. Some dominant wolf he was. Instead of dwelling, he tugged on the bond that centered him to his wolf. The bond ached like a sore limb, pulsating until finally his wolf listened and came forward. He barely remembered a time when the bond between him and his wolf didn't hurt. It had been different the first couple of times he'd changed as a child. That was before the demon had taken everything from him.

When wolves were children, the moon goddess spared the pain of shifting. Shifters didn't turn for the first time until they were two or three. Until they hit puberty, and sometimes for a few years after that, they didn't feel what the adults felt.

At least that was the case with most children.

Since the demon attack, Finn felt every single shift, every single arch of pain that came with transforming from a man to a wolf. Just as he felt it then.

Though the moon goddess had blessed the original hunter with the power to shift, it wasn't intended to be a blessing at first. The hunter had killed an animal in the forest for no reason other than joy, so the moon goddess had come to the earthly plane and forced that wolf's soul into the human's body. The human was forced to share his body with the soul of a wolf and learn how to control dual natures, as well as shift into the animal it had killed for sport. His cousin Parker was actually a descendent of that first hunter if the stories were true.

And because shifting wasn't intended to be a blessing, it *hurt*. Tendons tore as they gave way for bones to break in half and into pieces, altering their shape so they could make way for the new form of a wolf. If a shifter was made into a wolf after they were adult, they never had a chance to learn how to shift without the aide of no pain. Most threw up the first time, their bodies giving out at the unnatural way their bodies mutilated themselves in order to become their other half.

Finn's muscles tore along with the tendons and his face elongated into a muzzle. Fur sprouted along his skin before receding again. Each pore on his skin burned as the fur came through again, this time remaining. His legs turned to his back haunches, his feet turning to paws. His arms bent awkwardly to form his forelegs, strong and able to take the brunt of a jump and fight. While most of the wolves in his family and those in the Brentwoods could partial shift with their claws and fangs, most wolves couldn't. It was either or. Now his wolf was the chosen form, his body shaking as the transformation completed.

He threw back his head and howled. He wasn't in his den so no one answered back, but his wolf needed the freedom. While most of the time his wolf was silent, when he was in this form, he felt more of a connection than he did at any other time.

He turned at the sound of a whimper turned howl. Brynn was almost done with the change, and he stood over her, making sure she came out the other end okay. It was an odd reaction considering she was so much older than him and had been through countless shifts before his parents had even mated. She wasn't his, but right then, he knew he acted as if she were.

By the time she'd finished turning, her body shook, but she stood on four legs and held her head high. She was damn strong to shift as quickly as she had, considering he hadn't shifted that much faster than her.

While he was dark all over, she had rusty spots and streaks through her black fur. She wasn't as large as he was, but her stance held power. He nipped at her neck, surprising them both. That was a form of play, but usually only between lovers and mates.

She nipped back before darting to the side. She leaned down on her front paws and wiggled her tail in the air. If a wolf could smile, he'd have done so at the look on her face. She'd needed this, needed the connection to her wolf.

He yipped at her and she took off, running at full speed. He followed, the pads of his paws digging into the loose soil as they darted in and out of the trees. They jumped over fallen logs and large boulders, running as fast as they could. The wind tangled in his fur, and he lowered his head, hunting though not for any particular thing.

They continued on for almost an hour before Brynn finally stopped at another clearing close to where they'd begun. They'd gone in a large circle, and could have gone a little longer to go back to their clothes. It confused him that she didn't just keep going, but he stopped with her, shifting back to human as he felt the power of her transformation tug on his wolf.

The pain of going back to human hurt like a fiery hell, as well. Shifting again so soon took a lot of energy, and he'd have to eat soon to replenish it. Thankfully, both he and Brynn were strong enough to do it. He knew if they'd had to, they'd be able to shift again to head to their clothes, or worse, fight if needed.

As soon as he was back to his human form, his chest heaving and his sweat-slicked skin tender, he stood on two legs and frowned down at Brynn. He was exhilarated from the run, and his cock was rock hard not only from the adrenaline but also from the very naked, very sexy woman beside him. But he didn't know why they'd stopped here, and he wanted to know before he figured out what to do with the arousal between them.

Brynn finished shifting, her skin a blushed pink as she stood on shaky legs. She pushed her hair back from her face and raised her chin. Her eyes were bright but not wolf like they had been before. The run had helped, but he still felt as if he were missing something.

"Why did we stop here?" he asked. They were both naked, sweaty, and aroused, but he didn't do anything. Not yet. Not until he knew what she was thinking.

"I need to tell you something and I need you not to scream at me."

He blinked. "Why would I scream? When have you ever known me to scream?"

She huffed. "Fine. Don't growl or yell or shout. Sorry, I used the wrong word."

An eerie sense settled over his skin and he frowned. "I can't promise that...but I'll do my best."

She snorted. "I guess that's all I can ask." She let out a breath then met his gaze. "The reason I've been out of sorts, the reason I want to yell at you and yet want something more at the same time is for a reason." She paused. "I'm your mate."

Deafening silence.

What.

How.

No. That couldn't be true.

She was mistaken. That had to be the only answer to this because he didn't understand her words. She had to be joking. This was just a cruel taunt and a way to push him away because she couldn't stand him. That's all he knew. She *hated* him. Hated being around him. She pushed and growled and wanted nothing to do with him. She'd slapped him when he'd kissed her. She'd denied her attraction to him because he wasn't worth her time. That was the only explanation. He'd stayed away and not pursued because she wasn't his. His wolf hadn't told him. His wolf hadn't done a fucking thing. He hadn't wanted to one day meet his mate and yet have feelings for Brynn. He'd done *all* of that because he hadn't felt the potential mating.

This couldn't be happening.

All of these thoughts happened in a moment's time, all at once, crashing into him. He struggled to breathe, to think, to remember that he was the Heir and needed to remain in a form of control.

His limbs felt numb, his fingers tingling as if they couldn't quite keep the blood flowing.

He didn't say anything, but she continued.

"Or rather, you're mine. I can feel the potential bond with you. I've been able to feel it since before Gideon and Brie's mating. My wolf wants you, craves you. And the woman? She wants you, too. I've seen your strength, your compassion. But I know you don't feel the same. I know you want me because you're a man and you are attracted to me. But I know. I know that the moon goddess fucked up. Either your wolf doesn't want me at all and the mating is truly one-sided, or something happened and you can't feel it."

His mouth opened once, twice, but nothing came out.

Tears slid down her cheeks and she gave him a sad smile. "I know you're mine down to the very depths of my soul. I know that my wolf wants you with every breath she takes. Yet I know I'll never have you because you don't feel the same."

"Brynn..." he whispered.

She shook her head. "I know it's a lot to take in. I never told you before because I couldn't be weak. I couldn't open my soul like this, bleeding out in the open for you to take advantage and see me as nothing but a weak wolf. But it's killing me, Finn. I'd rather you know now, know my pain, than stand beside you in silence because I was too afraid."

He reached out for her, his fingers a breath away. He opened his mouth, but he didn't know what to say. It didn't matter though.

At that moment, the explosion burst near his ears and Brynn screamed. They both flew back as the wards rocked. The fire licked the wards but didn't come through.

However, the large tree that had been rooted for over a century on the other side of the wards cracked. The sound was deafening. He crawled in the dirt toward Brynn and brought her close, covering her body with his.

The tree that had once stood tall, its branches reaching far into the heavens fell on the wolf side of the wards, landing with a thundering crash.

Someone had bombed the outside of the den, and yet it was the bomb that had fallen just mere moments earlier that made his mind whirl. One word slammed into his mind over and over again.

Mate.

CHAPTER TEN

B rynn's body shook, but she didn't know if it was from the shock of the explosion or the fact she'd just confessed her deepest secret to the one man she shouldn't. She stood in her kitchen, another pair of shorts and tank thrown on as soon as she'd stepped inside. She'd handed Finn an extra set of sweats and he'd covered up, though he still stood shirtless in her dining room, looking as shell-shocked as she felt.

As soon as she could open her eyes when they'd been in the forest, she'd pushed Finn off of her. Both of them had jumped to their feet, claws at the ready. They couldn't see a single person near the wards, but they'd searched. Both had been bleeding and bruised from the debris, but it hadn't mattered. Her den was under attack, and she couldn't save them all on her own. Finn had risked his life for her people, and she would never forget the feeling of him by her side as they'd searched for the perpetrators.

Kameron and the men and women under his command had shown up soon after the explosion. Her Enforcer brother had felt something off a mere second before the bombing but hadn't been able to pinpoint its location fast enough.

No one had died. No one was hurt other than the scrapes and bruises Finn and she held on their skin. From the look of it, the bomb had been on a timer, the humans long since gone from that part of the den area. They couldn't even find their clear scents as the rain earlier in the day had washed it away. But she knew it was humans, just as the rest of them did. There was a feeling that wouldn't go away.

Her den had been attacked and there was nothing they could do because they didn't know who had lit the fuse.

Kameron had told her to go home and clean herself up, the curiosity in his gaze at Brynn's running partner blatant. She didn't answer her brother but she hadn't wanted to stand naked in a forest with the devastation of that section of the forest, her brother, and the man she'd revealed she held a potential mating for.

It was enough to push anyone toward a drink.

In fact, that sounded like a damn good idea. It would take a few bottles to get drunk thanks to her metabolism, but she could at least pretend the burn would lead to the numbness she so desperately needed.

She reached up into the cabinet and pulled out two tumblers and a bottle of whiskey. If she was going to drink, she might as well do it well and with the man in the living room. He might not stay beyond that drink, but at least she could say she tried. It felt as if an odd weight lifted off her shoulders but remained on her chest. She didn't know what would happen next, but she couldn't back away. Not anymore.

She padded into the living room, ignoring the twinge of the few cuts and scrapes she hadn't cleaned yet. Not smart, but she wasn't firing on all cylinders.

Finn stood in the living room, his hands on his hips as he breathed in and out. She loved watching him shirtless. The way his muscles bunched as he flexed made her mouth water. He had his back to her and she wanted to lick up his spine to lap up the salty taste of him. He was the epitome of strength and dominance, but he'd also let her lead earlier that evening. And he'd thrown his body on top of hers when the tree had fallen. He was a dichotomy of a more dominant male wolf, who was learning how to deal with a very dominant female wolf. He wasn't failing at it, but it wasn't as if they'd truly explored the opportunities because of what they weren't saying.

She'd told him that he was her mate, and he hadn't been able to articulate a complete sentence.

It wasn't fair to hate him for that as she'd had a year to wallow over the idea, and he'd only had a few seconds before the world literally rained ash.

"Drink?" Her voice held firm, surprising her.

Finn turned around and she about swallowed her tongue. The hard ridges of his abdomen stood out, glistening and so fucking lickable. The lines on his hips that led to his cock were deep grooves that begged her fingers to explore.

Not that she was going to do anything like that.

Her wolf pushed at her, sated from the run but still wanting more than just a glimpse of succulent flesh.

"You're bleeding." Finn's wolf wasn't in his words—honestly, she wasn't sure she'd ever heard his wolf in his words like so many others. But the edge of growl that laced his tone told her he hadn't settled from their earlier run. Good, because she was far from settled.

She looked down at the cut on her arm and the other on her stomach and frowned. "They aren't deep."

Finn shook his head and moved closer as if to touch her. She took a step back. They both froze.

"I...don't touch me. Not yet." Her voice didn't break, but damn it was close. She shook the bottle of whiskey in her hand. "Drink?" she asked again.

Finn studied her face, his brows lowered. "I need to clean you up first."

"You don't need to clean me up. I'm fine. They're shallow and will heal on their own in a couple of hours."

He let out a shaky breath of his own. "I need to clean you up."

Confused, she let him pass and watched him walk toward her kitchen where she kept a first aid kit. She hadn't told him it was there, but he could probably scent the antiseptic in the cabinet.

He came back with the kit in his hand and gestured toward the couch. "Sit and pour. I'll clean you up."

She raised a brow but did as he ordered. Normally, she'd bite back at his tone, but they were in such an odd place right then, that she wanted to be careful as to when to push back. She wouldn't be taking many more snapping orders, but she'd do this because at least he was talking to her. That was progress.

"You're hurt, too," she said softly as he sat on the coffee table in front of her. The piece was a large hunk of wood that could handle her brothers' weight so it didn't even creak when Finn had sat down. Her place wasn't the most feminine, but she couldn't really keep it that way with her family in and out of the rooms so often.

"I'm fine."

That was enough. She set the tumblers down, aware if she slammed them down as she wanted to, she'd shatter the glass and give Finn something else to patch up. She twisted open the whiskey and took a swig directly from the bottle, the burn down her throat helping. Finn raised his brows at her, but she didn't give him the bottle. She needed the burn to help her deal with a dominant wolf with the equivalent of a thorn in his paw.

She poured them each two fingers then handed him the glass. "Drink."

"You're still bleeding."

"Yeah, and I'll continue to until you fucking take the drink, Finn. Don't mess with me right now."

Finn growled low in his throat but took the glass before knocking it back. She took her shot as well and set her glass next to his on the table.

"Feel better now?" he asked, clearly annoyed.

Well, fuck him. She had been sweet and accommodating, but damn it, it wasn't like her to roll over all the time.

"No, I don't. But please continue to clean up the wounds that will take care of themselves later."

He gripped her arm and growled. "I *need* to do this, Brynn. I don't understand why I need to so badly right now, but I do. Understand?"

She froze, letting him wipe down her cuts. "No, I don't understand," she whispered.

He frowned and finished up cleaning the scrapes before setting everything to the side. "I'm your mate."

She swallowed hard. "Yes. At least that's what my wolf tells me."

He searched her face, his gaze tracking every inch of her it seemed. "And yet I don't feel the urge."

Her heart shattered, her soul aching for the loss of what she would never have. She might have known the truth, might have told herself over and over again it would never happen, but to hear the words laid out from his lips, she felt as if she would die.

And she didn't like the woman she would become if she allowed this pain to take over. She didn't want to crawl into the forest and curl up into a ball while she waited for the world to pass by. That wasn't who Brynn Brentwood was.

"I see."

Who owned that hollow voice?

Oh, yes, that was her.

Finn shook his head. "I don't think you do."

"What is there to miss? The moon goddess fucked up. My wolf wants you. After over a century of living, I've finally found the one man and wolf I could be with, and his wolf doesn't feel the same. Hence, fucked up."

She tried to stand, but he put his hands on her knees. She sat back down at the contact. His hands were so warm, so calloused. So freaking hot.

"It might not be the moon goddess," he whispered and she lifted her head.

"What?"

"It could be me. I'm broken."

Her hand shook as she cupped his cheek. The rasp from his beard went straight to the warmest places within her.

"What do you mean? You're not broken, Finn. You're...you're the Heir."

He gave her a sad smile. "Do you know what happened to me when I was a child?"

An eerie feeling slid over her. She shook her head. "I don't know everything. I know Caym and the Centrals attacked your den many times during the war."

"That's a way of saying it." He let out a breath. "I was three or so when Caym broke through the wards. He was trying to find his daughter, my aunt Bay."

Brynn coughed. "I...how did I not know that? Dear, goddess. She mated to Adam."

Finn frowned. "Yes. Bay is half demon, but she's wolf through and through. There is nothing different about her other than she spent most of her early life on the run because of the blood in her veins."

She winced. "I'm sorry. It just surprised me."

"It's not an easy thing," he said gently. "Caym broke through the wards and ended up landing in a clearing where we'd been relaxing for the afternoon. I happened to be running right next to him when it happened."

He met her gaze and she held her breath.

"He broke every bone in my body. I remember the pain, Brynn. I remember more than I should. I remember the screams. I remember people trying to reach me. I remember being awake when Caym dropped me to the ground with his power and turned to slit my uncle Josh's throat."

Brynn didn't gasp, didn't make a sound. She was afraid if she did anything like growl for the injustice of it all, Finn would stop talking and she'd lose him...more than she already had.

"Hannah, Josh's mate, was able to save us, but Josh will always speak with a lower register because of the damage to his vocal cords." He licked his lips. "She Healed me but sometimes...sometimes I don't think she fixed everything. Or maybe she didn't put me back together right."

"Oh, Finn," she cupped the side of his face and leaned forward, pressing her forehead to his. His breath warmed her face, and she sat there while his body shook.

"My wolf is so fucking quiet, Brynn. I can't always feel him. It's like he's there, but it's a haze. I don't have to try to control my wolf because while he might be quiet, he's *always* there. I'm never not fighting my wolf, but the damn thing won't speak to me."

"You're not broken," she rasped, tears in her throat.

Finn ran his hands up her side and she shivered. "What if I am? What if the moon goddess didn't make a mistake? What if my wolf is screaming at me that you're my mate, but I can't hear him?"

The horror at his statement made her pull back. Tears stung her eyes, but she couldn't cry. She blinked a few times, trying to breathe while she did so.

"No. That can't be the case."

"What if it is?"

Her heart broke once more. She hadn't thought it possible. The empty cavern that had once held her soul became a wash of pain that slammed into her over and over again as she tried to catch her balance.

"What does this mean?" she asked, her voice a whisper.

"It means that...I don't know, Brynn. Look at me." She opened her eyes, unaware she'd even closed them to begin with. "I've wanted you from the first time I saw you across the circle. I was a teenager then, but I knew you were someone I wanted. I didn't know what it meant, and maybe I still don't. But ever since then, I've wanted you. I've stayed away because I know once I have you, I'm going to become addicted. I crave you more than breathing, more than anything I could ever hope to have. I knew that if I had you, I'd keep you—

even if we weren't mates. I stayed away because that wasn't fair to you...or our future mates."

She winced.

"But...but I was wrong, wasn't I? I stayed away because I didn't want to hurt us, and yet, I did so anyway. I hurt you so much. I'm so fucking sorry."

He broke her; she didn't think she'd heal. Not when she didn't know what would happen next.

"What are we going to do?" she asked.

"I don't know," he whispered.

"How can we fix that? If your wolf won't speak up, or however you want to say that, how do we get past this? Because I don't know if I can go on and fight by your side and do what we must for our Packs if I have to see you and know I can never have you."

"What if you can still have me?"

Her hands shook. "How is that even possible?"

"What if we tried? What if we went through with it? What if we tried to mate and form a bond? Maybe it can still happen and it's only my wolf being silent."

Hope, sweet hope, slid through the numb.

"How can we have a future with no bond?"

"Humans do it every day."

"But we aren't human..." Life would be far easier if they were. Then again, she'd never have met him if she'd been human.

"Take the chance," he whispered, cupping her face. "Take a chance with me. If we try, if we mark each other and make love, our bond can still form. We don't know for sure it won't."

"How can you take that chance? How can you look at me and tell me that you'd risk everything without knowing for sure that you're my mate?"

Finn lowered his mouth to hers, brushing her lips for a mere moment before pulling back. "Because you, Brynn Brentwood, are worth any risk I would take, any pain I would feel. You are worth far more than a broken wolf."

A single tear slid down her cheek, and Finn used his thumb to brush it away.

In that instant, she knew she loved him. She had fallen for him and his strength by being by his side and watching him *live*. She could do this. She could try to mate with him and be with him without a bond in place.

And if she kept lying to herself, she could one day believe it.

It was the only hope she had.

"Try, Brynn. Be with me."

"Okay."

Finn's eyes widened for a moment before he crushed his mouth to hers. She moaned into him, pushing out thoughts of what could come and only thinking about the man she could taste.

He tugged on her hair and she gasped. She wanted more. *Needed* more. Her wolf howled, begging for a bond that might never come.

"I want you," he growled.

"Then have me."

He nipped at her lip then licked the sting. She raked her nails down his back and he shuddered.

"Bedroom. Now. I don't want to break your living room while I fuck you."

"Fuck me? Or make love to me?" Stupid, Brynn. Why did she have to say that?

"Can it be both?" he asked. He stood up, gripping her hips as he did so. He lifted her off her feet and she wrapped her legs around his waist.

"Then show me."

He kissed her hard then trailed his lips down to her neck. She moaned aloud, rocking her body into his as he made his way back to the bedroom. He'd never been back there before, but her house wasn't large enough for him to get lost in.

When he set her down on her feet, she did what she'd wanted to do before and licked up his chest. He growled low, the vibrations sliding along her tongue. She looked up at him then moved to bite down on his nipple.

He slid his hands through her hair and smiled. There was a promise in that smile. One that made her shiver.

"Do it again. And then I'm going to do the same to you."

Her nipples ached at his words. "Promise?"

"Promise."

She licked her way over his chest and bit down on his other nipple, loving the way he groaned at her touch. He tugged at her hair and she let her head fall back. He kissed her again, this time slowly as if he were fucking her mouth with his tongue. She gripped his hips, her thumbs digging into those grooves she'd wanted to trace before. He tasted of whiskey and heat, so hot and *hers*.

His hand slid down her back and cupped her ass, molding her cheeks in his large palms. She rocked into him, his hard cock pressing into her belly. She wanted him inside her, *needed* it.

His fingers traced under the leg of her shorts, slowly sliding back and forth, each stroke going higher and higher. She'd forgone panties so he had easy access.

Thank the goddess.

His thumb brushed along her lower lips and he growled, pulling away from her mouth.

"So fucking wet."

"Take me," she gasped, kissing along his chest. She let her hands explore down his front, cupping him through his sweats.

"Let me touch you first. I want to know every inch of you, taste you until I have your essence imprinted on my tongue. I want you begging for me, so wet you're dripping and can take me easy. Then I want to fuck you hard into the bed until we both come and fall into a heap."

Her legs almost gave out at his words. He gripped her ass harder, keeping her up. The action sent his thumb upward, breaching her ever so slightly. They both froze then groaned in unison.

"You're tight, Brynn."

"Then you'd better make sure I'm ready for you," she teased.

He bit down on her lip. Hard. He didn't hold back from her, didn't hold back that strength that made him who he was.

Good.

Because she wasn't about to hold back from him.

She let her claws slide out then reached around to grip his ass. "Make me come, Heir. Or I'll have to do it myself."

He licked his lips. "I think I can do that."

"Think? Poor pup. *Do* I need to teach you how to pleasure a woman? Let's see, you'll need to make sure I'm wet. To do that, you're going to want to play with my clit, pinch it between your fingers and maybe even your teeth. Don't be gentle. I want it rough. I want you to fuck me hard, Finn. Think you can do that, Heir?"

He had her on her back on the bed and her shorts on the floor in the next breath. She tried to catch her breath, but in the next moment, she had her hands tangled in Finn's hair as he licked up her seam.

"You're so fucking sweet," Finn growled against her clit and she almost came, forcing herself to hold back so she could take more of him. She didn't want it to end too soon.

He spread her thighs, licking her pussy like he couldn't get enough. The flat of his tongue took long swipes before flicking her clit. She shuddered, so close to release she could taste it. She gripped his head harder, and he hummed against her at the same time, sliding two fingers inside her, curving them so they hit her at the perfect spot.

Her back bowed off the bed, her body shaking as she came hard against his face. Pleasure shot through her, her limbs going numb before burning with too many sensations at once. Finn moved, hovering over her and stripping off her top as she came down. He must have taken off his pants at some point because he had his cock at her entrance, poised to take her.

She opened her eyes, licked her lips, and gripped his biceps. "Yes. Please. Now, Finn. Now."

He swallowed hard, a flicker of hope and fear mixing with the lust in his gaze. She lifted her legs and wrapped them around his waist. He leaned on his forearms around her head and kissed her.

Just a brush of lips, a sweet caress of promise and dare she hope...love.

She arched, and he entered her slowly, oh so slowly. He stretched her, his cock wide and long, perfect for her. It burned slightly, but she relished it. This was her Finn, *her* Finn. She had him inside her after far too long of watching him without knowing what would happen. She'd pined for him, and now she had him. She'd taken the risk, and she would never regret this. She couldn't. Not when she had the man she loved in her arms, deep inside her, connected like she had never done before.

He pumped in and out of her, their gazes never wavering. He didn't go slow now, no, he slammed into her at an ever-increasing pace as they went higher and higher.

"Finn," she whispered. She turned her neck to the side, and he groaned.

His fangs slid into her neck, marking her wolf as his. She waited for the snap of the bond, the pleasure that came with having him mark her.

It never came.

Instead of wallowing, she pushed away the agony of what she knew to be true and let him move her head once he'd licked the wounds. She met his gaze, saw the knowing inside, and choked back a sob. When her fangs elongated, she bit down on the juncture between his shoulder and neck, marking him as her own.

Finn was *hers*.

Damn the bonds.

Damn the broken fractures that a demon with no sense of life and love had created.

She slid her fangs back out and licked the wound, aware she only felt the love she had for Finn. The shocking lack of anything else brought her crashing down from any high she might have had.

Finn cursed then growled, sliding his hand between them both. "Don't give up on us, Brynn. Don't give up on me."

She met his gaze and let the pleasure of his words, of his touch, wash over her and she came with him. He filled her, body yet no soul. The second snap of the bond should have happened then, but the hollowness in her heart told her it hadn't.

Finn hovered above her, still deep inside her as he fought to catch his breath. She met the jade green of his eyes and knew what she should have known from the beginning. Or maybe she'd known all along and had lied to herself once again.

There was no bond.

There was no future with the man in her arms.

There was nothing.

CHAPTER ELEVEN

Finn slid out of Brynn, his heart breaking for not only himself, but also the woman beneath him. His body still shook from his release and the utter beauty of what they'd just done. He wasn't a romantic, wasn't a man who discussed his feelings beyond a certain extent, but he wanted to tell her everything, let her know exactly what he was thinking. He'd known she'd be special to him, that he'd become addicted once he had one taste.

But it wasn't just her taste.

It was *her*.

She was his, as he was hers.

Only his wolf wouldn't complete the bond.

Things would work out, he promised himself. They had to. Because he couldn't think of another outcome, not with the woman beneath him. Before he could hold her, bring her close and tell her everything would be okay and they would find a way to make their mating work, she scurried out from under him and crawled off the bed.

"Brynn." His voice didn't break, but it was damn close.

She turned her back to him, her body shaking.

"Don't." The tears in her voice broke him once more.

He sat up, his hands shaking. "Talk to me. Please don't go like this. Don't make me go. This can't be the end. We can try other things."

Brynn turned to him, tears on her cheeks but not in her eyes. The lack of emotion inside went through him like a sharp blade, deeper than any other tear or sob she could have shown.

She'd given up.

She was going to push him away.

He scrambled off the bed and cupped her face. "Please don't make me go. I love you." He knew it was the truth as soon as he said it. It wasn't a last ditch effort. It was his heart, his soul. He loved Brynn Brentwood, and now he was going to lose her. "I love you, Brynn. I want you. I want everything with you."

She blinked at him and bit her lip. "We can't. You don't have the bond, Finn. You can't feel it. I can't feel it with you either because it needs *both* of us. I'm dying inside. Can't you get that? Can't you see that every time we make love, every time you touch me, I'll need more? I'll just be reminded of the fact that we could have had something more and that I'm not going to get it. I don't know if I could go on knowing that we are so close to having everything and yet have nothing at all. I need more, Finn. More than you can give. It's killing me." Her voice broke, and he knew she was on the verge of tears. It was sheer will alone that she wouldn't cry just then. Not in front of him.

"I'm not enough," he whispered, knowing the truth of the matter.

She shook her head, her face bleak. "It can't be. Every time I'm near you, I break. I can't do that." She took a step back from him, naked, her eyes hollow. "I thought I could. I thought I could go on and be with you without the bond. But we're not human, Finn." She paused. "This wasn't a mistake. I will *never* regret this because if I did, then I'd die a little more inside. But I can't be with you and know there is no future. We can't have kids without the bond, Finn. We can't have a true mating. We can't be recognized under the moon with our Alphas. We are from two different Packs and don't have a bond between us. I've never felt your wolf, and now I know I never will."

He swallowed hard. There was nothing more he could do just then. He couldn't think, couldn't breathe.

Finally, he took a staggered breath. "I'll go, Brynn."

Her lower lip wobbled, and she nodded.

He took a step forward and placed a gentle kiss on her lips. That she didn't move back, told him that this was the end for her. "I love you." She didn't say it back.

And with that, he left.

Left the woman who should have been his, should have been bonded to him body and soul. The demon had broken him, twisted him up so deeply inside that he'd never stood a chance at a future with the one woman he loved.

The only woman he'd ever love.

She was *his,* and he couldn't have her.

Fate fucking sucked.

He pulled on his sweats and walked barefoot and shirtless outside, ignoring the looks and growls. His shoulder bore Brynn's mark, but no one would be able to feel a bond that wasn't there.

No one spoke to him as he got through the wards and went to his car. He drove in silence, his brain acting on autopilot. Somehow, he'd gotten it into his head that if he made it home, made it to the Redwoods, he'd find a way to make it work, or at least make it through the pain. He'd find a way to fix it all. But he wasn't sure he'd be able to find it.

His body shook, his sweat-slick skin growing cold in the cool air. He could scent Brynn on his skin, deep in his pores. He wasn't sure if he wanted it to wash away so he wouldn't be tempted by the agony of what could have been, or for the scent to stay so he would never have her gone from him in truth.

He just didn't know anymore.

He drove through the Redwood wards and made his way to Hannah's home before he'd even thought about where he was going. The Healer had saved his life once before, maybe she could do it again.

It was all he could think of.

He needed Brynn in his life, and now that he'd had a taste of her, he knew he'd never get over the addiction of her.

He loved her.

And had lost her.

"Finn?" Hannah stood next to his car. He hadn't even realized that his window was open. Or that she'd opened the front door and come to him. He gripped the steering wheel, his knuckles going white. "Finn, honey, what's wrong?" Her eyes widened, joy blending with the worry. "Is that a mark on your shoulder? Are you mated?"

"It didn't work, Hannah," his voice broke, tears falling down his cheeks. He turned to watch her face as the truth set in. "I'm broken, Aunt Hannah. It didn't work."

Her face paled and tears slid down her cheeks, as well. "Oh, sweet heavens."

She knew. She'd figured it out. Or at least had put a few pieces together. She'd worried about him ever since the attack, and now she had cause.

He was broken. Only, he wasn't sure there was a way to fix it.

"Hannah?" Josh ran out of the house, Reed on his tail. "What the fuck is going on, Finn?" He cradled Hannah close to him and Reed stood on the other side.

"We felt the bond pulse in agony. What happened?" Reed glared at Finn, but Finn couldn't find the energy to glare back. Not when he'd lost any hope of having what he'd thought would always come. Perhaps not all hope, since he was with Hannah just then, but enough hope that it hurt to contemplate moving forward.

"Don't yell at him," Hannah whispered. "Get him inside and call Maddox. Now." Her voice grew stronger with each word, and the men did as they were told. Finn wasn't sure he'd made the right choice by coming here. He wasn't sure he could stand to see a true triad working as a mating when he couldn't even make it work with one woman. One woman who held the strength of thousands.

"Come on, Finn," Reed said softly. "You look like you were beaten."

Josh was on the phone with Maddox as he led Hannah back into the house.

"I wish that were all," Finn whispered. "I fucking wish it was just a simple beating." He opened the car door, his limbs heavy. He tried to swallow, only to find his mouth dry.

"We'll take care of it," Reed said firmly, putting his arm around Finn's shoulders. "Let's get you inside, okay?"

Finn didn't answer but let Reed carry some of his weight. His heart hurt, and he knew Brynn had to be feeling worse. That just made it all crash down harder on him. It was as if he'd been knocked in the head with a two-by-four, his brain not fully catching up to what was going on around him. Reed set him down on their couch before squeezing his shoulder and leaving him to stare at the wall in front of him. Finn didn't like this numbness, the lack of ability to do anything but remember to breathe and pray there was a way out of this situation.

He wasn't normally this person. If there was a problem, he found a way to fix it. If there was a fight to be fought, he led the charge. He didn't like the fact that felt so defeated, was acting so dejected. If he didn't get his head out of his ass, he would lose Brynn in truth. She'd push him away harder than she already had, and he wouldn't even have the option of finding away to make their mating work.

What he needed was to fix the bond with his wolf. *Then* he could be with Brynn until the end of their days.

The world needed the two of them. Their Packs needed them. They'd be stronger together than they'd ever be apart. He'd seen that during the past year when they'd been working side by side on their mission. He might have thought she hated him, but it couldn't have been further from the truth. She'd just been trying to work out how she would stand next to him and know he wouldn't feel the potential bond he should. Or perhaps she didn't know that at all, maybe she though he just didn't want her. He couldn't blame her for her hostility toward him all this time, nor could he fault her for the mixed messages she'd sent recently. Everything had truly gone to shit and now he knew why.

Someone sat next to him on the couch and he inhaled their scent. Hannah. She didn't lean into him or even touch him. She merely sat next to him, letting him know she was there. She was an earth witch, not a wolf, but she was Pack. Her life was tied to Reed's as Josh's was through their mating bond. She'd been brought in as their Healer, and soon, she'd step back and allow Finn's brother Mark to hold the mantle.

He cleared his throat then looked down at himself. He smelled of Brynn and sex, only wore a pair of sweat pants, and had a fresh bite mark on his shoulder. It probably looked as if he needed his head examined since he'd come to their place first, rather than his own home. But he hadn't thought of going to his place with Charlotte. There was nothing she could do but try to help him through whatever this was. But Hannah had Healed him once before. It might not have taken as it should have, but there had to be something she could do now. If not? Then he wasn't sure what he'd do next.

All he knew was that he'd walked out of Brynn's place to let her breathe because he would do anything to keep from hurting her. But that didn't mean he'd given up on her. She'd given up because she'd already had a year to work through this, a year to die a little more inside. This was new to him, but damn if he'd give up right. He couldn't.

"Drink this," Reed said, and Finn looked up. "It's just water," his uncle continued. "After you rehydrate, we'll get you the harder stuff if you want it."

"And it looks like you might need it," Josh said from the other side of the room. The former human, now half-demon, crossed his arms over his chest and frowned. "You want to tell us what happened? Or do you just need to sit and be with family? We're fine with whatever."

"What my knucklehead mate means is, do you need anything?" Hannah asked, her voice soft. "What can we do for you? We love you, Finn. Do you want us to call your folks? Call Charlotte? Or even Brie?"

Finn shook his head then gulped down the water in one go. The cool liquid soothed his parched throat. He hadn't realized how dehydrated he was until he'd finished the glass and found himself still thirsty. Reed handed him another glass he hadn't seen in his uncle's hand, and Finn drank it a little slower.

"I wanted to come here because...well, because that's what my brain did when I went into autopilot." He shrugged, knowing he was being vague and that he had to get into specifics. The more he thought about it though, the more he thought he might have made a mistake by coming here. Hannah was a gentle soul, even with the powers and strength of a warrior earth witch. She might have guessed part—if not all—of what had happened to him, but stating the words outright would hurt her.

He'd made a mess of everything, but now he needed to move on and work through it because Brynn deserved better than a broken wolf and the heavy absence of a mating bond.

Hannah reached out and gripped his hand and he squeezed hers back. "Tell us what happened, Finn. We won't call anyone you don't want us to, but Maddox is on his way." She tilted her head. "In fact, there he is now."

Finn had, of course, scented his uncle before she'd even said anything about him. Maddox walked in without knocking and made his way into the living room, taking a seat on the coffee table in front of Finn.

"I headed off the rest of the family," Maddox said softly.

Finn let out a sigh. "They felt everything through the bonds, then?" he asked, knowing it was too good to be true to hope that he'd protected his family from his own worries.

Maddox shook his head. "Quite the opposite, in fact."

Finn sat back, frowning. "What?"

Hannah squeezed his hand. "We don't feel *anything*, Finn. It's like you've been cut off completely. If it weren't for the fact that you're here and I can now feel a muted presence of you, I would have thought..." her voice caught "...I would have thought you'd died or left the Pack."

Finn sucked in a ragged breath, stunned. "I'm still bonded to the Pack, right?" He rubbed a hand over his chest, trying to connect to his Pack like he had before. He was the damn Heir. He couldn't just cut everyone off when he felt like shit. The Redwoods needed him to be strong. Brynn fucking needed him to be strong.

He closed his eyes and focused on the connections that kept him sane. All at once, warmth burst through his limbs and he coughed, the bonds fully pulsating again.

Maddox coughed, as well, and Finn opened his eyes. "You were connected before, just muted. Some couldn't feel you at all, and that scared the shit out of them. You're back, but damn, Finn, what happened? Why did you shut yourself down so hard emotionally that you disrupted the balance between yourself and the bonds that hold us together?"

Finn let out a breath then began the whole story. "I found my mate...but my wolf doesn't recognize her."

With each layer, each detail, Hannah grew more despondent while her men tried to soothe not only her, but Finn, as well. Maddox narrowed his eyes and did his work as the Omega, pulling in some of the pain Finn felt. But Finn only let his uncle do that for a little while before pushing him off. He needed the sensation, needed to remember how it felt to know he might never have what he thought he would. Without that tactile sense of loss, he'd lose focus.

Brynn was his focus.

The Pack and their future with the humans came next.

But those two ideals together wound into an array of dissonance that he had to work his way through. He couldn't have one without the other. He couldn't save his Pack, his people, without Brynn by his side. He didn't know why he knew that, but it was a truth to him. A truth he had to reconcile with the facts laid in front of him.

"I don't understand why Brynn can feel the bond, but you can't," Josh said once Finn had finished. "It was different for me and Hannah when it came to Reed. We aren't wolves, so we didn't get that connection right away. But with two wolves, I thought it was a sense of knowing, even if it took time. I see you're marked, and I am going to guess that she's marked, as well. But you're telling me it didn't work?"

Finn blew out a breath. "We tried. We convinced each other that maybe my wolf was just...for lack of a better word, masking what I should be feeling. But I know, deep down in my soul, that she is mine. My wolf might not be telling me this, but I know it. There's no way around it, and I'm not fucking crazy. She's mine, and yet my wolf is broken. I'm broken."

"I'm so sorry," Hannah whispered.

Finn let out a small growl. Her men growled back—even the non-wolf, Josh. "Stop it. You are not to blame."

Hannah's eyes filled with tears. "But I am, somewhat. Right? I've always known something was off since that day in the clearing. I've done my best to ignore it, to think about the fact that you're healthy and breathing, but I was wrong. And you've known it, as well."

He closed his eyes for a moment then met hers. "You saved my life. Caym broke every bone in my body, yet you saved me. You put me back together."

"But I didn't put you back whole. Or perhaps I didn't put the pieces together correctly."

"You saved the both of us," Josh snapped. "You risked your life and drained your energy and powers to save that little boy." Josh stalked toward his mate and pinched her chin, forcing her gaze to his. Finn would have growled, but the deep and everlasting love in Josh's eyes held Finn back. "I was supposed to be your protector, but I wasn't enough. I was supposed to get Finn out of the way, but I couldn't. Caym slit my throat, but *you* saved my life. *You* saved Finn. You do not get to blame yourself for *anything* that happened that day. *Anything*."

Finn frowned. "I'm missing something. What else happened that day?"

Josh winced, and Hannah closed her eyes. Reed cleared his throat but answered for them. "Hannah lost the baby she carried that day."

Finn choked out a watery gasp. "Goddess, no. Oh, fuck. Hannah, guys, I'm so fucking sorry." He held onto Hannah's hand as her men kissed her softly. Finn let out a breath as Maddox pushed his powers out, soothing the hurts that had long since passed but never fully faded.

"Caym took more from us than most of us will ever fully know," Maddox said softly. "But he is gone, and he cannot win everything."

"I don't know how we will fix this, but we will," Hannah vowed. "The new generation might be gaining their powers and taking over, but *we* started this and we will finish it. I refuse to believe that we have lost. You will have your mate, Finn, no matter what I have to do in order to make it happen."

"Within reason," Josh growled. "I will not have you hurt again."

Most days, Finn forgot that Josh wasn't a wolf. He was, in fact, an ex-Seal. Sometimes there truly wasn't a difference between the two when it came to his Alphaness.

"I don't want you to weaken yourself for me," Finn added.

Hannah raised her chin. "I won't be weakening myself. I will be working to find a way for you to get the happiness you so deserve. I'll do everything in my power to make that happen. Mark, Walker, even the other witches in our Packs. I won't give up, Finn. I should have known something was off all these years, but I've done my best to ignore it for fear of what I would find if I looked too close."

Finn ran a hand over his face. "I've ignored it, as well. I've always known my shifts were different, that my wolf was far too quiet and didn't push me like others. But I thought I could live with that. Fuck, I *could* live with that. I can't live without Brynn."

"The Redwood Pack Heir and the Talon Princess," Reed muttered. "We sure know how to mate into the Talons with a splash." His mouth twitched, and Finn shook his head, smiling.

"I love her, guys. I love everything about her. From the way she protects what is hers, to the way she stands by Brie's side. She doesn't have a true place within the Talons, and she's always blamed herself for that, but I think the moon goddess had a different plan for her."

Hannah's eyes widened. "I hadn't thought that far ahead. When you become Alpha, she would be the Alpha female of the Redwoods. That's...that's interesting."

"That's one word for it," Josh muttered. "We've all been through hell, and with the way the world is turning after the Unveiling, I have a feeling we aren't out of the woods yet. But I'll stand by my mates' side and find a way for you to have your Brynn. I won't deny you the happiness I have now. We'll figure it out, Finn."

"We have to," Reed added. "I will look through the texts and talk to the elders. It's what I have always done and will continue to do. You are not alone."

"You can't hide this from the family, nor the Pack most likely, but we won't let you struggle on your own," Maddox voiced. "You've sacrificed much for us, and are the public face of our Pack. You are never alone," he repeated.

Finn leaned on his family for a few more minutes before he abruptly stood, the scent outside surprising the hell out of him.

Hannah gave him a small smile. "It seems your family won't let you be alone, no matter how much you'd like to hide away from what has happened. Tell them everything, Finn, but first, do what you need to do to find the peace you crave. You will have your Brynn, this I promise you."

He hugged each of them then walked to the door, taking a deep breath as he opened it. The Jamensons were closer than any other family he knew—though he was coming to find out the Brentwoods were a close second. Over time, he had a feeling the Brentwoods would be as close, if not closer, because of the different kind of past they'd survived.

However close his extended family was, his immediate family was even closer. They knew his pain, though they didn't know the reasons. And for that, he would love them until he ceased to walk in this world.

His parents, Kade and Melanie, stood on the porch, their hands clasped and their faces filled with the love that had raised him through wars and the Unveiling. All of Finn's siblings stood behind them, their own faces a mix of curiosity and sheer determination. Gina, Mark, Nick, Drake, Tristan, and Ben were his past, and would be part of his future. He wanted Brynn here. He wanted her here to see this, to see his family and their strength.

"Let's go for a run," Kade said softly. "We will run as a family, as a unit. And when you are ready, we will hold you when you fall, and prop you up when you need us to."

"I don't know everything that has happened, Finn, but I will stand by you. We will all stand by you," Melanie whispered, her eyes filling with tears, though the power within showed. She was not weak. His family had long since taught him emotions and tears were not a sign of weakness, but showed the true soul of another and their ability to heal within a family and Pack.

"Thank you," he whispered then moved toward them. They all enveloped him in a group hug, some only able to put a hand on his arm or back, but they touched him, showing him that he was not alone, despite the fact that his wolf made him feel that way.

He would shift and run with his family. He would take each broken bone, each tearing of a tendon. Because if he did that, he would at least feel that pain, feel that connection to his wolf. He didn't have what the others had, but he would find a way to live through it.

He had his family, his Pack. And soon, he would have his mate.

Because there was no other way he would survive. Brynn was his future, his faith. And one day soon, he would have that bond. He had the power of hope when it came to the fate of his family.

He'd fight himself bloody for his future, his Brynn.

And soon, she'd know that.

Soon.

CHAPTER TWELVE

Brynn had acted rashly and without thinking. She knew that. And yet she'd pushed Finn out of her arms, her bed, her *life* because she'd been afraid of taking a leap and a chance with him. She'd thought she would be able to handle the emptiness, but instead, had panicked. She knew that if she'd just thought for a moment, she'd have been able to breathe. Just because they didn't have a bond, didn't mean they couldn't work it out. Plenty of wolves had done so in the past and had somehow made it through.

Those wolves, however, weren't in the same position she and Finn were.

In those pairings, neither felt the urge to mate, but over time, developed a bond between them. In her and Finn's case, it was horribly different.

And, of course, if she kept dwelling on what had happened, that would be the only thing she did for this lifetime. She didn't know what would come next with Finn, but for now, she needed to take a shower and actually find a way to be the Alpha's sister and not someone who wanted to be curled into the fetal position and cry until there were no more tears. She was already far too close to the latter for comfort.

While she didn't want to wash Finn's scent off completely, it was too much right then to have him on her in the potency it was. Her wolf could barely think with Finn in her pores.

She quickly showered, not lingering since she didn't want to stop moving enough to think. If she just kept going, kept working on the next part of her life, then she'd be fine. If she paused for too long, then her mind and heart would take over, the helplessness would get the better of her.

As soon as she pulled on a pair of jeans and a tank, someone knocked on her front door. For a moment, an agonizingly precious moment, she thought it was Finn. Then she inhaled and scented Ryder.

Of course, it would be Ryder. The others in her family would have been able to feel her wolf if they were of the hierarchy, but it made sense it would be Ryder who showed up. It wasn't that she was the closest to him, as she felt as if she were close to each of her siblings and cousins, but he was the only one who knew the truth about her relationship with Finn. Or at least knew what had come before she'd given in to the temptation of a future that would never come.

Enough.

She ran a hand through her wet hair and went to open the door, doing her best to keep her emotions out of her eyes.

From the look on Ryder's face, it didn't work.

His gaze traveled to the bite on her shoulder and his eyes widened. He met her gaze once more with an expectant look.

"It didn't work," she muttered. She would not cry. She'd done enough of that already.

Ryder stepped closer, his arms outstretched. "Come here, little sister."

She sank into his arms, wrapping hers around his waist. He closed the door behind them as she rested her cheek on his chest. When his arms hugged her tightly, she almost broke, almost let more tears fall, but she held strong.

She'd been the one to push Finn out of the house so she would have to deal with the consequences. Crying about it wouldn't help anyone.

Ryder patted her back awkwardly then moved back, his brows furrowed. She held back a snort since it wasn't the right time to laugh. Her brother did well with the hugs, but sometimes, it was as if he had no idea what to do with the emotions inside of him. Of course, she couldn't blame him since she was in the same boat. Their father had fucked them over in more ways than one.

"Do you want something to drink?" she asked, her voice raw. "I need some tea."

"Add some honey to it, Brynn. Your throat needs it. And I'll take a cup since you're making it."

She shrugged but started heating the water using her teapot. There were faster ways to make tea these days, but nothing tasted as good as her old pot that had gotten her through hell. Ryder got the cups down and the jar of honey while she looked through the tea leaves to pick what she wanted. No bags for her.

"Are you going to tell me what happened?" he asked once he'd sat down at the breakfast bar, leaning on his forearms.

"I already told you." She pointed to her neck. "It didn't work."

"Your way with words knows no bounds," he said dryly. "Now tell me. *What* didn't work exactly?"

She closed her eyes, took a deep breath. "I told Finn about the mating. Told him everything." Well, not *everything*. If she hadn't kicked him out, she'd have told him everything about her—about her past, her fears, her needs. But she'd lost him before she'd truly had him. That wasn't solely on the moon goddess. Brynn held her faults, as well.

"And?" He cleared his throat. "From the mark on your throat, I take it something happened."

She didn't blush, but it was close. "He looked broken and told me why he thought he didn't feel the bond." She ignored the pain in her heart. "We decided to try the mating anyway. Figured maybe it would work even if he didn't feel the pull I did."

"But it didn't work."

She shook her head. Thankfully, she didn't cry. The teapot whistled, and she started steeping their tea. "It was...it was the best thing I've ever felt. And yet the worst thing, since I knew there should have been more."

Ryder didn't look put out that his little sister was talking about sex, but she didn't want to dwell on it and make him uncomfortable. No use in both of them feeling that way.

"Then what happened?"

"I freaked out and kicked him out of my bed." She met Ryder's gaze as she set his cup in front of him. "I couldn't deal with the fact that we had no true future. We'd be able to make love but never have what we should. So I made the decision to end it before we could hurt ourselves more than we already had."

Ryder gripped her wrist, giving it a squeeze before leaning away. "And you regret that?"

She shook her head, paused, then nodded. "I think I made a mistake, but I don't know what to do about it."

"It's never too late, you know. If he tried to come to you before, knowing he wanted to have a future with you no matter what, he might have left to give you space. Finn isn't that bad of a wolf."

High praise from a Brentwood.

"I don't want to talk about it anymore. Okay? Tell me about Franklin's family. Are they doing okay? What about the case? Any leads? Are we any closer to finding out who attacked Franklin and Seth? What about the man who tried to run Finn and me over? "

Ryder studied her face for a moment then sighed. "Franklin's family is mourning. And before you start to feel like it's your fault, know that they don't blame you. They *know* you kept him alive for as long as you could. So stop with the blaming. As for the case, we're cold. Finn got the description of the car, but it was stolen. We don't know who did it. It could have been extremists. Could have been random humans with a grudge. Or, it could have been something far deadlier and connected to the government. Washington's been oddly silent since we came out. They're positioning their chess pieces at the same time we are, but I don't know if we're forming the right strategy for their attack."

Brynn let out a breath then took a sip of her tea. The honey soothed her aching throat.

"I feel like we're missing something."

"I feel the same way. We've done our best to protect our people, but until we know what the humans plan on doing, we can only keep at molding the public's perception of us while not allowing others into our dens."

"And that doesn't feel like it's doing anything productive." Her wolf growled at that. She hated feeling helpless. But until they knew what the humans had planned, they had to act as if things were normal. One wrong move and the powder keg would blow.

Ryder drank the last of his tea before putting the cup in the sink. "I don't know what to tell you. We're in a holding pattern that makes me feel helpless as hell, but we're going to find a way to keep the Pack safe."

"And my duty?" she asked. "Do you still want me to remain the face of the Pack? To act normal?"

Ryder leaned forward and brushed a kiss on her brow. "You'll find your path, little sister. And if that path is with Finn, then you will find a way. If not? Then we will be here to hold you when you need us. As for the face of the Pack? Gideon is holding off on that until we see what the humans' reaction to the attack is. So far, it's been...positive, for lack of a better word."

Her brows shot up.

"They saw you and Finn try to save your friends. People are shocked that anyone could be gunned down like that in broad daylight. Turn on the news when you have a chance. I know you've been in another head place recently with all that's going on, but when you're ready, come back to the duty you have."

She hugged him tightly then watched him leave, shame filling her. She'd been so caught up in her own pain; she'd stepped away from the real world. There had to be a better way to balance it. Her brother Gideon had done it. So had countless others. She wasn't alone in finding a mate—though she knew her situation was uniquely heartbreaking.

Determined to focus, she closed the door as someone knocked. She opened it, not bothering to scent who it was, and froze.

"Finn."

He'd changed into jeans and a henley, his hair wet from a shower. It would have annoyed her that he'd washed her scent off, but she'd done the same thing.

"Brynn." He cleared his throat and stuffed his hands in his pockets as if he were unsure what to do with his hands. "I know you told me to go, and I did, but can I come in?"

She backed up without a thought, wanting him near despite the actions that had moved her to tell him to leave in the first place.

"Why are you here?" she asked, her voice emotionless.

He faced her, his hands still in his pockets. "I left because you told me to, and I will *never* do anything to hurt you, but I couldn't stay away, Brynn. Not with so much between us."

She swallowed hard. "It hurts to be with you, yet at the same time, its agonizing *not* to be with you, Finn."

His jaw clenched, and he pulled one hand out of his pocket to cup her cheek. She didn't back away, and it took all within her not to lean into his touch.

"Take me as I am, Brynn. Take my soul, my body, my everything. We *will* find a way to form the bond." He let out a breath. "I talked to my Aunt Hannah, the one who Healed me all those years ago, and she is going to look for a way to fix my wolf. My whole Pack will help if needed. We're a family, and I will beg them if I have to." He met her gaze and her heart raced. "I'll go down to my knees right now and beg you to give me a chance if that is what you want."

She shook her head. "You should bow and beg to no one, Finn Jamenson."

"You aren't no one. You are worth more than the dominance of a wolf who lost a chance with the one woman who completes him. We will find a way to have the bond we deserve. You will have the mate you deserve. I will fight until my dying breath to make that happen. You deserve so much more than a broken wolf, but I want you, I need you, I adore you. Please, Brynn. Take me. Love me. Be with me."

His thumb caught a stray tear, and she sucked in a shattered breath. She hadn't even been aware she'd let that tear fall.

It was a risk. A huge step where she might end up dying alone and in pain, but the agony she currently faced, the emptiness she felt without him in her life was too much to bear alone. She may not have the bond, but she'd have *him*.

That had to be enough.

At least for now.

And if there were a hope for something her wolf craved, then she'd hold on to that hope with all her strength.

"I love you, Finn," she whispered, knowing he needed the words just as much as she did. His eyes widened, and she cursed herself for not saying it before when he had. Only then, she'd been backing away from the chance of something more, and hadn't wanted to add to the hurt with words of love.

Now though, she couldn't hold them in.

"I love you," she repeated. "And yes, yes I'll take a chance. I shouldn't have pushed you away, but I needed time to think. I went about it wrong."

His body shook, but he didn't move closer to her. "You didn't go about it entirely wrong. I mean, we don't know what we're doing here. We're in uncharted territory, but we'll figure it out. Just like we'll figure out the problem with the humans. Together. Because, Brynn? We are so much stronger together than we ever were apart."

She reached out and traced her finger over his heart. "So we'll be together, with no bond? What does that mean exactly?"

He gripped her wrist with his free hand, and she reveled in his touch. "That means I am yours as you are mine. I will never be with another, and you will do the same. I will love you until my last breath, and I hope you do the same for me."

"Of course," she whispered.

"We will figure out what it means for us within the Packs, but for now, we are one. We will figure out what to do about the bond, but until then, but we'll do everything like we're a mated pair." He met her gaze, pleading. "Please, Brynn."

She licked her lips, watching the way his chest rose and fell. "I can do that. I know you don't feel the same pull I do, but you're here. That means you either want to feel that pull or it's something different for you. Either way, you're *here*."

"We'll make it work."

She leaned forward and kissed his chest. "Yes. Yes, we will." Because there was no other option.

The hand cupping her cheek tilted her head back, and he crushed his mouth to hers. This wasn't a soft, hesitant kiss. No, this was *everything*. All the rage, the lust, the time they'd spent away from one another because they didn't *know*... Brynn kissed him back, biting his lip hard when he wouldn't open for her.

He growled, reaching around to smack her ass. "Watch the teeth, princess."

"You're with a dominant wolf, *prince*, better get used to my bite." She sank her teeth into his lip again, and he picked her up by the ass and slammed her back into the wall. She huffed out a breath but wrapped her legs around his waist as he pressed his body against hers.

"Oh, I know you're all dominant." He licked her lip, suckled, and then trailed his tongue up to the back of her ear. He rocked his jean-clad cock against the valley between her legs, and she moaned. "I want your claw marks down my back, your fangs in my skin as you lose control. I want you wet and ready for me to fuck you hard against this wall. Does that sound good to you, princess?"

To answer, she let her claw slide out of her fingertip and ripped his henley down the seam. He shrugged out of it, a grin on his face and his eyes still that jade green without the gold rim that told her his wolf was near. His wolf wasn't up front, not like hers, but she didn't care. She had *Finn*. And for now, that was all she needed.

He moved one hand and did the same to her shirt as she'd done to his. The coolness of the air against her skin made her shiver, but the heat from Finn warmed her right up.

He held her up with one hand on her ass, and she pressed her back to the wall so he could look his fill.

"Like?" she asked, her voice breathy.

Finn licked his lips then pinched her nipple. She gasped, arching into his hold. "Fuck, yeah. I didn't get to look my fill last time. We went so fast, I didn't get to properly worship you."

She smiled, her hands running down his arms. *Dear goddess, his arms.* Thick cords of muscle under scarred skin. He was a warrior. *Her* warrior.

"Worship me after. Fuck me first. I want you in me, Finn. Please."

He grinned then leaned down, sucking her nipple into his mouth. She moaned, rocking into him, and he teased her with his tongue and teeth. He released her with a pop then licked along the underside of her breast before laving his way to her other nipple and repeating the action. Her panties were drenched, and she was so close to coming from his play with her nipples alone, she couldn't breathe.

"Finn..."

He growled against her, and she stiffened. Her back bowed and her eyes slammed shut, waves of pleasure and heat hitting her with such force she would have fallen if Finn hadn't held her up. Finn growled again, keeping her coming until she was sure he would have to tear her out of her jeans.

When he set her back on her feet, she gripped his shoulders, keeping her balance. Finn had their jeans ripped off in seconds, his claws oh so careful with her skin.

"Goddess, you're fucking fantastic."

Finn laughed at her words then had her slammed against the wall again and inside her in one stroke. They both froze, his cock so thick and hard inside of her, she knew she'd never felt this full...at least not since earlier with him in her bed.

"You're pretty fucking fantastic, too, princess."

She reached around and gripped his ass hard with her claws. Finn sucked in a breath, his smile going wide and a bit feral.

"Fuck me, prince."

Finn kept one hand on her ass, the other cupping her face as he slowly worked his way in and out of her. The exquisite torture of his touch made her want to scream and moan at the same time.

"I'll make love to you, princess. And I'll fuck you at the same time." He kissed her softly then slammed home.

She gasped a scream as he pistoned into her, his cock going deeper with each stroke. She moved her hips with his thrusts, wanting him as deep as possible.

"Come for me, Brynn. Squeeze my cock and milk me."

She kissed him, her wolf rising to the surface, reaching for the other half of her soul that she prayed would one day be there. Finn moved again, this time arching in the perfect way to make her come.

Her inner walls clamped down on him, and he groaned, filling her up as he came with her. He leaned his forehead against hers, his body shaking.

"Love you, Brynn," he whimpered, "my warrior princess."

She grinned at the nickname. "Love you, too, warrior prince. My Finn."

It wasn't perfect, it wasn't a mating, but it was her new life. She had Finn by her side, and no matter what happened, she'd take the next step in her future with her head held high.

There wasn't any other choice.

****

Finn stretched, his body sore from his night with Brynn. He couldn't help the grin on his face at the thought of her. Oh, he hadn't slept well and was dragging ass right then, but he didn't care. He could scent Brynn on his skin, and while he felt the slight pang of disappointment that he couldn't feel her in his heart, he had her everywhere else. It would be enough. For now.

He trusted Hannah and the others to help him make Brynn his mate. The Redwoods had fought the impossible before. And damn it, he knew they would do it again.

He'd much rather be with Brynn at her place, or even at his, but instead, he'd had to come to his father's house to talk about a new development with the Pack. He wasn't sure what it was, but when the Alpha summoned, you came.

His mother smiled widely when Finn walked into the house, though he saw the worry in her eyes.

"You look happy," she said as she hugged him tightly.

He leaned down and hugged her back, needing the touch of his family even if he were happy.

"I am."

She moved away and searched his face. When it looked like she saw what she needed, she nodded. "Good. Brynn is strong, intelligent, and beautiful." She winked. "Good enough for my baby boy, I suppose."

Finn snorted and rolled his eyes. "Thanks, Mom." He sobered. "You know it's not official yet."

She thinned her lips and nodded. "I want to kill that demon, even after all these years for what he did to you. I have faith in Hannah and the others to find a way for you to truly mate with Brynn. Until then, do you think she will become a Redwood? The lines of our Packs are growing thinner with each mating, but the bonds are still with an individual Alpha."

Finn let out a breath. "I'm the Heir. I will always be a Redwood."

"And she doesn't have a place secured within the Talon hierarchy." Melanie frowned. "But without the mating bond..." His mother trailed off then shook her head. "We're getting ahead of ourselves. You *will* mate with her, and she will become a Redwood after that. Brie did the same for Gideon, and Quinn did so for your sister, Gina."

He didn't say anything. They *were* getting ahead of themselves, just as she'd said.

"Finn."

He looked up at his father's voice and let himself relax. His parents loved and supported him, no matter what. He had that to rely on, even as shit hit the fan.

"What's up?" Finn asked. "You said there was a new development. Is it about Seth? Is he okay?"

Kade nodded. "Seth is fine. Or at least as fine as he can be after waking up to discover Franklin didn't make it. Maddox and Drake are working with him, but healing from something like that isn't easy."

Finn wasn't sure his parents were aware they'd reached for each other as Kade had spoken. His parents were more in love now than they had been thirty years ago.

"What we actually wanted to talk to you about were the witches."

Finn frowned. "Huh? The witches? What about them?"

Kade gestured toward the couches, and Finn took a seat while his parents sat across from him.

"You know the witches are just as much in hiding as we once were," Kade said.

"Yeah, some are out, but humans don't truly believe it." Witches had been persecuted in every century—burned at the stake, drowned, murdered for being different. Some were out in the open, but humans didn't truly understand their natures. Wolves mated to humans and witches just as much as wolves. In fact, his sister Gina was part fire witch thanks to her birth mother, and his Aunt Hannah was an earth witch.

"True enough. But the witches are restless." His Alpha met his eyes, and Finn sat still. "They will be unveiled soon, Finn. Either on their own terms or by those that know too much. There is no hiding for them while we are out."

Finn cursed. "We knew it was an eventuality."

"Yes, but they are reaching out for help."

"What do you mean?" They were on good terms with some covens, not all, but they'd worked with them in the past. Their wards were created not only by the moon goddess, but the witches within their Packs, as well.

"With the attack on Seth and Franklin, the one on you and Brynn, and the bombing near Talon land, things are getting hot. And yet we still don't know if and how they are connected. We can't survive on our own, and neither can the witches, not if the humans bring a full-on war to our doorsteps."

Finn sucked in a breath. "So it's the paranormals versus the world?"

Kade shook his head. "We don't want it to be like that. We want to be able to move freely as we always have. But with the attacks on our wolves and the other attacks on Packs around the country? We're at a precipice. One I hope to the goddess we don't fall over."

"What do you want me to do about it? There's a reason you asked me here."

"We're forming another taskforce. This time with the witches. We're going to have our Heir and Omega meet with the witches and ensure we end up on the right page. The Talons will be sending Ryder and Walker, as well."

Finn nodded. "That makes sense. Are we using Drake or Maddox?"

"Drake," Melanie put in. "Maddox has a lot on his plate and will one day be able to fully hand over the mantle of the Omega."

Finn raised a brow. "Does that mean I don't have a lot on my plate?"

"You do, and you'll have more as time moves on. We all will."

Finn stood and raised a hand over his face. "Let me know when we're meeting. I need to get back to Brynn."

Kade lowered his brows but nodded. "I'll send over what I have, and the four of you can work everything out. I trust you." His father stood, studying his face. "When you're ready to talk about Brynn and have her meet us in a more formal way, let us know. We'll figure it out for you, son. We will."

Finn ignored the ache in his chest and nodded. "Thanks," he said roughly. He wanted what his parents had. Damn if he'd let fate not let him get it.

He left the house and got in his car, quickly shooting a text to Brynn letting her know he'd meet her outside the wards for lunch. Him going on Talon land too often would be an issue until they'd planned their unique way of mating. He would have called, but he knew she was in a meeting with her brother Max about a council issue and didn't want to distract her any more than he already was. After all, she was distracting him, as well.

By the time he got to their meeting place, he was on edge with wanting her. He didn't even need to be inside her, damn it, he just wanted her near. He *knew* this was the man in him, not the wolf, but he had to pray that the wolf was somehow getting through, even if it were a bare whisper.

He stopped the car and got out, a smile on his face as he spotted Brynn.

She stood under a tree, her eyes closed, her face tilted to the sky. She was a goddess. So fucking gorgeous he could barely breathe.

Unable to help himself, he gave a wolf whistle.

Her eyes still closed, she flipped him off.

He threw his head back and laughed.

Then the world exploded.

RYDER

Ryder didn't speak as his Alpha and brother, Gideon, spoke of his new duties as a taskforce member for their work with the witches. The silence wasn't all that uncommon. He didn't speak often as it was. He was the quiet Brentwood. Of course, most of his siblings and cousins were quiet. They'd been through hell. What more did they need to speak about?

Gideon spoke softly to Walker about one of the pups that had found a thorny bush earlier that day while Ryder sat back and did what he did best.

Thought.

He'd ally with the witches if his Alpha asked him to. It would be for the good of the Pack. And as the Heir, he held the power to make some decisions in Gideon's absence. He knew he wouldn't be Heir for long since the title would go to Gideon and Brie's firstborn son—or daughter, considering how the moon goddess liked to keep changing the rules.

For now, though, he would help his brother with the overwhelming task of being an Alpha wolf to a

Pack that hadn't quite healed, in the middle of a war that no one knew if they were truly fighting.

They'd lost one of their own recently, and Ryder knew it wouldn't be the last.

And while all of that was happening, he knew he was missing something. What, he didn't know, but there was something off about whom he was and what he was supposed to do.

Would working with the witches help? Again, he didn't know, but he would do as he was told. That's what he did best. What he was told.

Until, of course, he knew that he had to do something else...something to save his Pack and his people.

Kameron slammed the door open and ran into the room, his wolf in his eyes. All three wolves already there stood up, ready to fight.

"What is it?" Gideon growled.

"There was an explosion outside the wards."

Ryder frowned. "Again?"

Kameron let out a growl of his own. "Yes, and we can scent Brynn and Finn like before." He met Ryder's eyes and a chill slide down his spine. "They weren't there. Someone took them. I'm sure of it."

"Two bombings around them is not a coincidence," Walker drawled, his voice deceptively calm.

"No. It's not," Gideon agreed, Alpha to the bone.

"We'll find them," Ryder vowed. "Call the Redwoods. Someone took our Pack, our sister. We'll go for blood."

His words didn't surprise anyone. After all, he spoke when it mattered.

His sister was in trouble, and the humans better pray that she and her mate made it out alive. Because if she didn't? The lines of war wouldn't be so blurry.

No, the lines would be drawn and filled with blood.

The Talons didn't let anyone hurt their own and live.

And Ryder knew that deep in the dark valleys of his soul.

CHAPTER THIRTEEN

Either a two-ton pickup had rammed into her, or Brynn had been blown up by a bomb. From the way her body ached and her eyes refused to open, she wasn't quite sure which. She held back a moan as she forced herself to wake up. As she didn't know where she was or what had happened, she didn't want to make any excess noise and alert someone of her presence. If that were even the case.

Her eyes opened slowly and she tried to take in her surroundings. Darkness surrounded her, but her wolf eyes could at least make out some shapes. Metal bars, a dirty floor, and a low ceiling.

A cage.

She was in a cage.

Pushing away the memories that threatened to boil over, she inhaled deeply. Rot and blood overwhelmed her senses, but she pushed past it and tried to scent where she was. She could only see that she was in a dark cage, nothing more. Her other senses, however, went into overdrive.

There.

She knew that forest scent of man and strength.

Finn.

She slowly rolled to her belly, placing her hands on the dirty floor. The coolness of metal beneath her palms surprised her, but it shouldn't have. This was a full-on cage, not just a prison cell.

Her wolf rose to the front, and she tried her best to make out shapes in the darkness. If there had been more than a slight sliver of light, she might have been able to fully see. As it was, she could barely figure things out.

She squinted at one blurry shape in particular and sucked in a breath.

Finn.

The shape wasn't moving, but if she focused, she could hear the slight intake of breath, the slow beat of his heart.

Her wolf whimpered, but she didn't make a sound. Finn was alive, most likely hurt, but alive. Speaking of being hurt, she quickly assessed her injuries and wanted to curse. Dried blood matted her hair to the back of her head, and she felt a few scrapes and bruises over her skin. Other than that, she wasn't really injured. Whatever had blown them up in the forest had knocked her out cold so someone could pick her up and bring her to wherever she and Finn were now.

It couldn't be a coincidence that she and Finn had been near *two* bombings right outside the wards. The first had to have been a practice run to test the wards.

The second was to take them in.

Brynn couldn't scent anyone other than Finn and humans near the cages, so she had a feeling that the war that wasn't quite a war had escalated.

The shadow in front of her moved, and she bit her lip, trying not to call out to her lover, her mate.

She watched the shadow as it moved as if to assess its injuries and surroundings before finally turning toward her.

Praying she wouldn't alert anyone who could be watching, she reached through the bars toward the shadow. She was only guessing Finn was in a cage, as she couldn't quite make out the bars, but she wouldn't be surprised if that were the case.

The shape reached out for her, and she strained her arm through the bars, her shoulder pressed tightly against the opening.

Their fingers didn't touch, but she felt the brush of air against her skin as Finn tried desperately to reach for her. Her heart lurched. So close, yet she couldn't feel his touch, couldn't feel *him*.

Overhead lights clicked on. The harshness burned her eyes, and she blinked twice so she could focus. Finn met her gaze, his green eyes intense. Quickly, she took in his appearance, noting every single cut and bruise.

Someone would pay for hurting him.

Finn gave her a nod, and they both moved their arms back and slowly turned to whoever walked toward them. Their footsteps were light, but she could hear the muted taps along the floor as the human came closer.

"You're up," the man noted. "Good. I was afraid the blast had knocked you out too hard. It would suck if you died right away. Our plans didn't account for that."

Bile rose in her throat at the thought of whatever plans the human in front of her had. And *they*? How many were there? Where were they? And how the hell were she and Finn going to get out if they were locked in cages? But the human had said they hadn't accounted for their deaths...so maybe they hadn't accounted for other things, as well. Hopefully, she and Finn would be able to use the humans' lack of understanding of wolves to get out of there.

She prayed the humans underestimated the wolves.

Because if they hadn't?

She and Finn were screwed.

The man walked forward, and Brynn studied his face. It was one of the men from the car that had tried to run them over. The same man that had threatened her in broad daylight with unspeakable things. He looked like some backwoods criminal—his head shaved, spotty ink running down his arms, crooked as hell. He wore a leather vest over holey jeans and seemed to have forgotten his shirt. The cut he wore wasn't of a local or national MC, but rather a wannabe one. It was evident the man had seen too many movies about what to look like if he wanted to be a delinquent, but that didn't matter. He still had her and Finn in cages.

He held the upper hand.

For now.

The man frowned at them then gave a nod. "I'll be back in a few minutes so we can begin the fun." He rubbed his hands together then turned toward a door she hadn't noticed before. He paused then turned back, his brows lowered. "Fucking animals like you shouldn't walk this earth, you know. You're a mistake, a blight on humanity. Only you aren't human, are you? We're going to cut you open and see how you tick. Then we're going to kill all of you. Once you're gone, we can go back to being normal. Because you *aren't* normal. You're beneath us, and it's about time you learn that."

With that, he stomped away, locking the door with a loud click behind him.

Her pulse raced, and she let out a small growl. "I can't believe that idiot caught us," she said quietly. She couldn't see any cameras in the small room they were in. In fact, other than the two cages and the lone door and light, she didn't see anything.

"I have a feeling he and his buddy have help from an outside source," Finn said softly.

She turned to him, her eyes wide. "They're extremists. Who would help them?"

Finn snorted, his jaw clenched. "Anyone who wants us out of the picture. Think about it. Extremities have received help through many sources over time. This is only the beginning."

Brynn let out a breath. "I know. I *know* that. I don't know why I'm not thinking clearly. I'm older than you. I've seen way more shit than this, and yet my brain is slow right now."

Finn immediately rushed to the side of his cage closest to hers, gripping the metal bars. "Are you hurt?"

She shook her head and winced. "Damn it. I think I have a concussion. I should be fine soon, but it's muddling up my thoughts." She met his gaze, her face set. "I need to get over it if I'm going to help us get out of here."

"I'll kill them for daring to hurt you."

"I already promised myself that I'd kill them for putting bruises on your skin."

Finn flashed a feral smile. "This is why I love you, dominant female of mine. And Brynn? We're going to get out of here. There's no way they can keep us forever, not when you and I can get out of this. Plus now they have *two* Packs after them." Finn let out a low growl. "They fucked with the wrong wolves."

She smiled back, though she knew she didn't look happy. "Damn straight." She ran a hand over her bare arms and held back a shiver.

"What's wrong?" Finn asked. "Other than the obvious."

This was her mate—bond or no—it wasn't as if she could keep secrets from him. "My father used to keep us in cages like this. He'd wanted to see how much we could take before we broke."

Finn growled, this time louder than before. "I'd kill him again if I could."

She shrugged. "Gideon took care of that for us, though I wish I had been able to help. We took out our uncles since they were the ones helping him. But our father's betrayal as Alpha hurt our Pack for a long time. We're just now really whole again, and now look what's happening."

"The Talons are strong, Brynn. Anyone can see that. And as for this cage? We *are* getting out of here."

She reached for him once more, their fingertips a breath away as he reached for her, as well. "Damn it," she muttered.

"I'll hold you once we're out of here, princess."

"I know you will. As for getting out of here? First chance we have, we break free." She met his gaze. "You leave me behind and get help if you get free first."

Finn snorted. "And you're going to leave me behind if the opposite is true? I don't think so. We're getting out of here together. No sacrifices. You get me?"

She sighed. "I get you." She wouldn't have been able to leave him anyway, but the thought of having him hurt made her want to howl to the moon.

The door opened again, and this time, two men came in. She leapt to her feet though she couldn't stand fully. The other man raised his arm, shooting what looked like tranquilizers toward the cages. She growled and rolled out of the way of the first dart, only to be hit by a second. There was only so far she could roll away inside the cage. The dart pierced her skin and whatever was in it slammed into her body quickly.

Fuck.

She met Finn's eyes and they each growled.

Someone had found a way to sedate wolves. Finn had been right. These humans weren't working alone.

Her head hit the bottom of the cage as she passed out, praying she'd wake up again.

Only when she woke up, she almost wished she were back in the cage. The humans had strapped her and Finn to separate tables so they were forced to look at each other. The tables were on an incline, so it was as if she and Finn were almost standing. Thick metal bars and straps across their legs, hips, torso, chest, and forehead held them in place.

The human that had shot them with the darts stood between them, an odd smile on his face. "Thanks for joining the living, Brynn Brentwood," he drawled. "I wanted you awake for this."

She screamed as the man went to Finn's table, a large blade in his hand. Finn met her gaze, his eyes narrowing as the human cut into Finn's flesh. The butcher made two long cuts down Finn's stomach, the thin trails of blood following made Brynn's stomach heave.

Finn's jaw clenched at each cut, but he didn't scream, didn't let out a sound. The fucking humans had to know that having her watch would be another form of torture.

The doctor finished up his cuts and turned to Brynn, a puzzled smile on his face. He wiped Finn's blood off the blade using his white coat, forcing more bile to Brynn's mouth.

"Let's see if female wolves bleed the same as male ones do."

"Are you really done with me?" Finn asked, his wolf in his voice. Her mate's wolf didn't come out often. This couldn't end well.

"I'll be back to you soon," the doctor said, not letting his gaze leave Brynn's. "Now, you screamed for him, will you scream for yourself?"

She raised her chin as much as she could, considering she was strapped down. "Fuck you."

"I don't do animals, but my partner might." He licked his lips then stabbed her in the hip. Not a slice, but a deep fucking stab that she was sure scraped the bone.

A whimper threatened to break through, but she held it in, even as the fiery agony of the deep cut raced through her system. Her wolf slammed into her, wanting out, wanting blood, but she couldn't shift while locked up like this.

Finn growled, screamed, and cursed as the doctor slid the blade out of her skin and stabbed again, this time a little higher. Black spots danced behind her eyes, but she refused to pass out.

The doctor tilted his head, as if studying her reaction then slid the blade back out once more.

"Interesting," he mumbled.

"Fuck. You." A trail of blood slid out of her mouth and she wanted to scream. He'd cut her deep, and for some reason, she wasn't healing. Neither was Finn now that she thought about it. There had to be something on the metal of the blade or in the tranq they'd given them earlier. Hell, this wasn't good. Not only for them, but for whoever the humans caught in the future.

The game had changed once again.

This wasn't magic, this was *science*. She could feel it in her wounds.

The doctor held the blade up to her eye and she tried to pull back. "I wonder if you would be able to shift without an eye. Of course, you would, but your wolf would only have one eye. Right? Or would it have two? I wonder..." He shook his head. "Soon. For now, just this."

He cut into her face, a single slice down her cheek. She screamed then. She broke, the pain intensifying with each passing moment. Finn howled, an agonizing song that turned into the crunching of metal.

The doctor flew back, the knife landing next to his body. Finn broke the man's neck then went to Brynn. Bruises and cuts marked Finn's body where the bands had been. He still had the long cuts on his stomach, leaving blood trails as he moved, but he seemed to ignore them. He'd broken through the metal by shear force, and she knew he had to have internal bleeding because of it.

"He cut you," he growled, his voice more wolf than man. "He won't hurt you again." With that, he let his hand turn to claws as he pulled at the metal encasing her. It creaked and groaned, breaking in his hands. "Can you walk?" he asked, his hands now human and pressed against the wound on her hip.

Pain flared and she tried to nod, only to shake her head. "I think he broke my hip." Her eyes widened. "How did he do that with just a knife?"

"There was something on that knife, Brynn. We're not healing. Fuck." He turned and pulled out some bandages from a drawer, pressing them to her hip and face. She winced, trying to help with his wounds, but he wouldn't let her. Damn man. Yes, she was worse off, but she *needed* to help him.

"You can help me soon, princess. Okay, I'm going to carry you on my back. I can't carry you in the front and still fight. Hopefully, by the time we get out of here, you'll be healed a little bit more and we can shift. I just don't want to use up the energy to shift now."

She nodded, wrapping her arms around his neck and climbing onto his back when he turned in front of her. She kissed his neck above the mark she'd left, which seemed like years ago.

"We don't know how many people are out there, and we don't have a weapon."

Finn grunted, his hand on her thigh. He moved toward where the knife lay on the floor and picked it up. "Hold this. We need it analyzed anyway. We're getting out of this, Brynn."

"I know, Finn. I trust you."

"Back at you, love."

Her body ached, and she was rapidly losing blood, but with Finn by her side, she knew they would win this. There wasn't another option.

****

Finn opened the door with Brynn on his back. He could feel her slipping into unconsciousness, even with the knife in her hand, and he held back a curse.

"Give me the knife," he whispered.

She handed it to him, her movements slow, measured. She was fading fast, and he knew he needed to get them out of there. Under normal circumstances, both of them would have been able to walk way from this easily. Only she'd been knocked out twice, forced to remember her father's own brand of torture, and sliced up even more than Finn had. With whatever coated the blade, they'd been hit hard. He'd get his mate out of this and get her healed because there was no way he'd lose her because of some random elitist human shits.

Finn inhaled, the coppery scent of her blood hitting his nose. He shuddered. Damn it. Those cuts were *deep*.

"You okay, princess?"

"Let's just get the fuck out of here, prince."

It didn't escape his notice that she hadn't answered his question.

Beneath the scent of her blood, he only scented two humans. The dead one behind them, and the one that had been part of all of the other alterations. It was interesting that he could only scent two, but that didn't mean they weren't working with others outside the building they were in. From the look of the walls, it looked like an old, abandoned warehouse, but Finn didn't know much more than that.

He had no idea where they were, or how far from help they'd been taken. Brynn needed a Healer. *Now*.

Footsteps echoed, and Finn held back a growl. The stench of the other human came closer, and Finn gripped the knife in his hand.

"Hold on," he whispered to Brynn sub-vocally. Only a wolf would have been able to hear him. The human wouldn't know he was there.

The human came closer. The bastard's eyes widened and he fired a shot toward Finn and Brynn. Finn ducked out of the way, Brynn still on his back, and then went closer to the human who'd taken too many breaths.

He sliced the fucker's throat before the guy could shoot again. The human dropped the gun, and thankfully, it didn't go off. He gasped then fell to the floor, clutching his throat.

"You should have let him live, we would have gotten something out of him."

Finn cursed. "They hurt you," he growled.

"I know. They hurt you, too. Damn it. Okay. We will find another way. Now, let's get home." Her words slurred at the end, and he pulled her closer to his back before running as fast as he could to the door the human had come through.

Finn found himself outside in a forested area he couldn't recognize. "I don't know what land we're on." If the humans had been stupid and brought them to the wrong Pack's land, it would be another pain in the ass to deal with.

"Brynn?"

She didn't answer.

"Fuck." He kept going and blessed the moon goddess when he found an old Jeep that reeked of the dead humans. He quickly put Brynn in the front seat and checked her pulse. It was weak, but she was still alive. He kissed her forehead then slammed the door and ran to the other side. It was an older model vehicle, so he could at least hotwire the thing. Any newer and he'd have been fucked.

He slammed on the gas and sped his way down the road, praying he could recognize a major highway or landmark. They'd taken his phone when they'd kidnapped him and Brynn, but the car had a communication system so he could make a call as soon as he knew where he was. He reached over for Brynn's hand and gave it a squeeze. She didn't squeeze back, but he could feel her pulse. She was alive. For now.

As soon as the road ended, he saw the major highway and let out a breath. They were close to the

Redwoods. Thank fuck. He dialed his father's number using the on-call system as it was the first number that came to mind.

"Yes?" His father's voice was a growl, the wolf so close to the surface that Finn could practically scent it.

"Dad."

"Finn? Thank the goddess. Where are you? Are you safe? We're coming to get you."

And just like that, Finn almost relaxed. He couldn't, not with Brynn unconscious and bleeding by his side, but his father's voice and strength meant everything.

"I'm on my way to you. I'm about twenty minutes out. I'll talk about everything when we get there." His voice broke. "Brynn's hurt, Dad. Bad. Can you call the Talons and have them send Walker to you? I'm closer to you than them. I'm afraid if I keep going to their den I'll lose her." He let out a breath. "Maybe Hannah and the others can at least help with some of the wounds while we wait for Walker to Heal her."

Kade paused. "Your mother is calling now. We'll take care of your mate. Get her here. Get yourself here. We'll help you and then we'll find whoever did this and make them pay."

"The two who did it are already dead."

Kade growled. "Good. But we don't know if it was just the two of them."

"No, no we don't." Finn frowned. "Have Reed and the others come, too. And some of the Talons, if they can. I have a knife that we need to look at. There's something on it that's not quite right. It's not magic. I don't know what it is, Dad. And they used tranqs on us that actually worked."

"Fuck. Meet us at the clinic. Get here, son. Get here."

"We're on our way."

He sped his way down the highway, knowing he was dangerously close to getting a ticket, but he didn't care. This was Brynn's life. His torso ached, and he knew he'd need some Healing of his own, but that would just have to wait.

When he drove through the wards, he didn't slow down. Brynn's breathing slowed with each passing minute. He slammed on the brakes in front of his uncle's clinic and jumped out of the Jeep with it still running. He went to Brynn's side of the vehicle and opened the door, pulling her into his arms. She'd soaked the front seat with her blood, and he held in a growl. He needed to be strong for her, and freaking the fuck out because of the sight of her blood wouldn't help anyone.

His uncle North, a doctor, ran toward him, Hannah and the others on his tail. "Walker and the Talons are almost here. They were on their way to us anyway when you called. Give her to me, Finn, and let's get inside."

Finn growled. "I've got her." He pushed past the others and stalked into the house, Brynn's body shaking in his arms. Finn set her down on one of North's medical beds and moved back but kept his hand on hers.

North and Hannah came in with Mark at their side.

"Take care of her first," Finn gritted out. "Do what you can until Walker gets here."

Hannah went to him and pulled him away. He reached for Brynn, but his aunt was stronger than she looked.

"Mark and North will do what they can. Let me look at you."

"Help her. Please." His wolf whimpered—the first time he'd heard that sound in ages. Damn it. Why couldn't he be normal?

"They are. And I need to Heal you. You'll both be whole, and then we'll move on to the next thing. You aren't doing your mate any good bleeding on the clinic floor like this."

He looked down and sighed. Blood oozed out of his wounds but he was so numb from seeing Brynn like she was, he could barely feel the pain now.

"My helping you won't hurt her, Finn."

He met his aunt's eyes and nodded. "Okay," he whispered. "But Hannah? She's not my mate yet. I can't *feel* her. I only know she's alive because I felt her pulse. It's killing me."

"They found a way, son," Kade said from the doorway. His father came close and gripped Finn's face between his large hands. "They found a way," he repeated. "But first, I need to know you're okay."

Finn felt his mother at his side, her hands on top of Hannah's as his aunt Healed him. It might have been the Alpha female aiding the Healer with power, but he thought it was more of a mother helping her son. Warmth spread through him as his wounds knitted back together.

"How?" Finn croaked. "How?"

"You'll have to die, Finn," Hannah whispered. "Just like you did as a little boy. You'll have to die so we can put you back together again."

Finn blinked then looked over at his mate. She hadn't woken up, but the blood had stopped pouring. His body went numb at his aunt's words.

Death.

He'd always known he'd died that day.

Fitting he would have to die again.

But without the connection to Brynn, he knew he'd feel like he was dead anyway. She was worth more than anything, even his life.

"Do it," he whispered. "Kill me."

CHAPTER FOURTEEN

"**N**o. You can't just kill him." Brynn paced inside the clinic, her hands on her hips. Walker had come to Heal her when she'd been unconscious. Thanks to whatever chemical was on the blade, it had taken a lot of energy on all their parts. Her face Healed quickly, but her hip took so much damage that she'd forever hold a scar.

A scar to remind her of the day she'd almost lost her mate.

And she'd be damned if she'd lose her mate again.

"Its not a true death."

Finn's words brought her out of her thoughts and into the present. She flipped him off. "Fuck you. You don't get to die to try and see if you can fix your wolf. We're not doing that. We'll find another way."

Finn stopped in front of her, halting her pacing. "If it allows me to be with you in truth, then I will gladly die. They'll bring me back."

Brynn growled. "No."

"Do you think I want my son to die?" Kade, the Alpha, asked. "Do you think this is an easy decision?"

"It's not yours to make," Brynn snapped.

Kade growled low, which made her brother Gideon growl back. Great, now there was an Alpha asshole challenge to deal with.

"Brynn," Finn whispered. "It's my decision."

"It should be *ours*," she said. She knew she sounded petulant but damn it, she couldn't allow him to be hurt. Because the solution wasn't just him dying. No, he had to die the exact way he had before. They'd have to break every bone in his body once again and kill him so Hannah and Mark with Walker acting as an anchor could pull him back into the land of the living. Hannah was older now, more experienced. And everyone trusted she would be able to fix the bond that had been tattered between Finn and his wolf.

And once that happened, he'd be able to mate Brynn.

It so wasn't worth it.

"It's not happening," she said softly. "We should be worrying about who took us. Not this."

"Brynn," Gideon growled. "We are worrying about that, and dealing with it. But right now, you and Finn need to mate correctly. It's going to fuck up the Packs if you don't. You know it. You ran away from him before because of it."

Brynn sucked in a breath and glared at Ryder. "Traitor." She'd voiced her fears, and her brother had told the others.

"They needed to know," Ryder said with no shame. "But listen to Kade, will you? Oddly enough, this isn't all about you."

"What?" she asked, confused as hell. Why did everyone know more than her? She hadn't been out of it for that long, had she?

"Like I said, I don't want to hurt my son," Kade said somberly. "But it's not only about your mating. If his connection isn't right with his wolf, it might have hurt his connections to the Pack, as well."

She met Finn's gaze and wrapped her arms around his waist. He hadn't put a shirt on from before, and she could still see the slightly puckered new skin forming over his wounds.

"Is this true?"

"I don't know. I've never been the Heir without having the thread to my wolf be...off. If I can help my Pack more by doing this, if I can save my people? Of course, I'd do it. But, Brynn? You are it for me. I'd do it for you in a heartbeat."

The words washed over her and her hands shook. "I...I guess it needs to happen, then." She didn't hold on to hope that things would work. As long as Finn made it out alive, that would be all that mattered. A mating bond between her and Finn would only be second to the breath in his lungs as far as she was concerned.

Finn cupped her face and gently brushed a kiss over her lips. "I love you."

"I love you, too." She held back tears. She wouldn't cry in front of these people. The only one she would cry in front of now was Finn. He was her rock and she hoped she was his. "I don't want you to hurt."

Finn gave her a sad smile. "I think it's inevitable."

Brynn shuddered out a breath. "So when does this happen?"

"Now," Hannah said, her voice strong. For a woman who was about to kill Brynn's mate, she looked remarkably calm. That was, of course, until she looked into the Healer's eyes. Hannah was breaking inside, and Brynn had a feeling if this hadn't been Finn, she wouldn't have done it. Hannah was trying to right a wrong she hadn't truly committed, and it was hurting everyone.

Brynn let out a breath and pulled away from Finn, keeping her hand in his. "Hannah. You didn't do this. Caym did. I know that, and I bet you everyone in this room does, as well."

"Damn straight," Josh growled. He wrapped his arm around Hannah's waist while putting the other firmly around Reed's.

"But she knows that, doesn't she?" Reed added.

Hannah rolled her eyes at her mates then nodded. "I know that. It doesn't absolve me of the guilt I feel, but I know it was the demon that did this. Now I'm going to fix it." She raised her chin. "*We* are going to fix it. And if it brings Finn even more into the Pack and allows him to help our people with more power? Then all the better."

She flexed her fingers and nodded at the table. "Lay down, Finn. We're going to do it all at once. Each of the dominants in the room will break a bone, maybe two. However they can hold on to you and do it so it's as quick as possible. It won't kill you, not fully, but then we'll have North send you over the edge with a cocktail of drugs that works on wolves. When you're gone..." her voice broke. "When you're gone, Mark and I will Heal you, but better than before. Walker will guide us since he doesn't have the bonds to you that we do, but as Healers, we have our own ways of acting as anchors."

Brynn blinked as the small, curvy woman spoke of breaking bones and killing Finn in a medical manner. The woman was Finn's aunt; family, and Pack, and spoke of it as if it were nothing. The strength inside Hannah for her to be able to do that was astounding. Brynn admired her all the same. Even if her wolf hated her just a little bit for what she had to do.

Finn kissed her again, this time hard. "I'm coming back."

Brynn refused to let him go. "I'm not leaving the room, Finn. I'm going to be here during it all."

"You don't have to watch this."

"Yes. I do. I need to. I need to be here for you. Don't ask me to leave because I won't."

Melanie came to Brynn's side and gripped her hand. "I'll be with you. I...I can't break my baby," she whispered in Brynn's ear.

Kade came to them, his face solemn. "I'll stand by the two of you, as well. My wolf won't allow me to do what needs to be done."

His words weren't a sign of weakness, but rather one of strength. He loved his son, his Heir, so much that he couldn't hurt him—even if it were needed.

Finn kissed Brynn once more then nodded at his parents. "It'll be okay." When he went to the hospital bed and sat down, Brynn thought her wolf was going to jump out of her skin and kill anyone who dared touch her mate.

Kade positioned himself in front of Melanie and Brynn, an odd look on his face. "Remember this, Mel? I seem to remember having my brothers hold me back when you were changed."

Melanie closed her eyes and put her hands on her mate's chest. "I remember. I remember you screaming for me. I don't want to have to scream for my boy, Kade."

"It's okay if you do," Brynn said softly. "I'll be screaming." There was no use lying.

"And that's why I will hold you both back. Our Finn will be strong." There was a promise in Kade's words that allowed Brynn's wolf to breathe. This man would soon be her Alpha if things worked as they hoped. He was a good man. But right now, all she wanted to do was make sure Finn was okay.

"Get into position," Hannah ordered. Mark stood by her side near Finn's head. Walker stood behind them, his hands on both of their shoulders. Gideon, Ryder, Mitchell, Josh, North, Cailin, Logan, Maddox, and more of the Redwoods and Talons crowded around the table. Each of them put both hands on a different part of Finn's body, bracing themselves.

Goddess. They were really going to do it.

They were going to break him.

A growl that ended on a whimper slid from her lips, and Kade put his hand on her uninjured hip. "Hold," he whispered.

Melanie made a similar sound and leaned into her mate.

"Ready?" Hannah asked, her voice steady, though Brynn couldn't see the other woman through the mass of bodies.

"As ready as I'll ever be," North whispered.

The others nodded in assent.

"Now!" Hannah called.

The sound would forever haunt Brynn's dreams. Each wolf moved at once, breaking the bones in their hands. It echoed off the walls, in her mind, and in her heart. Finn called out once then went silent. Brynn screamed and pushed at Kade, who held on to her, strong. She pulled her gaze from the mass of bodies to her mate's Alpha and glared.

She kept pushing until she truly saw the wolf in his eyes and the grey hue to his skin. This was killing him just as much as it was killing her. That was his *son* behind him.

Fuck it all.

"Move back," Hannah called out. The group surrounding Finn moved as one. Brynn watched their faces. Each looked sick, ashen, and ready to vomit.

Good.

"North. Do your thing," Hannah said softly.

North swallowed hard, and Brynn pushed at Kade, her wolf in control.

"No!" she screamed.

"Hold," Kade whispered, his voice a tad weaker than before.

North jammed a needle into Finn's skin, and Brynn broke free of Kade. She knew the Alpha had let her go. She was no match for him. But honestly, it was too late. The beat of Finn's heart slowed.

Slowed some more.

Then stopped.

Finn was dead.

Gone.

Lost.

Hannah began chanting, her arms outstretched over Finn's upper body. Mark's lower register joined her in the chanting, though his hands held steady over Finn's head. Brynn gripped Finn's hand, begging him to come back. Come back to her.

"You can't die on me fully, Finn Jamenson. I'm going to kick your ass if you don't come back."

"She means it, too," Mitchell murmured.

"Come back," Melanie whispered.

"Come back," Brynn repeated.

She waited.

She didn't know how long, but she waited. Hannah kept on her feet, her mates holding her up at the end, with the others holding Mark and Walker up. Finn never moved. Never twitched.

His hand grew cold in hers.

He had died.

Not just a little death, not partially dead.

Truly dead.

She threw her head back and howled. Others joined her, but she wasn't sure who it was—a mix of Redwoods and Talons.

Finn's hand twitched in hers.

Brynn swallowed hard and looked down, willing Finn to wake up. "Wake for me, Finn. Open your eyes so I know you're there. Come back to me."

His eyelashes fluttered, and Hannah moved back, passing out from exhaustion in her mates' arms. Mark and Walker leaned on others as that group left the room, their attention on those who had risked their lives for her mate. Brynn only had eyes for the man she loved.

His eyes snapped open. "Brynn." His voice was strong, not as if he'd just freaking died in front of her.

"Oh, thank the goddess." She leaned down and captured his lips with her own. Finn's hand went to the back of her head and he deepened the kiss. She let out a surprised moan before pulling away. "Finn?"

He sat up, looking fully Healed. His eyes glowed gold. "My wolf. I can *feel* it. I can hear him. I can feel you, Brynn. Holy fuck. Is this what you've been feeling all this time? How the hell can you manage?" He slid off the table and kissed her again, only to break away when someone cleared their throat.

"I take it your bond to your wolf is stronger?" Kade asked.

"Yes. I can...I didn't know how much I was missing." There was an awe to his voice she hadn't expected. She put her head on his chest, the strong heartbeat under her ear soothing her in a way she hadn't thought possible.

She cupped his face and smiled. "You came back."

"I'll always come back for you."

"You two need to heal a bit longer before you can finish your mating," North said dryly. "I know the mating urge is strong between the two of you, but you need to hold off. You just died, Finn, and Brynn is still sore from the attack."

Finn growled and quickly picked Brynn up, setting her on the table. "Your hip? You need to sleep. Let me get you a blanket." He closed his eyes and took a deep breath. "Shit. My protective tendencies were always strong, but now with my wolf pushing, it's even worse."

Brynn smiled. She couldn't help it. Her wolf was so fucking happy. Finn's wolf was *strong*. And theirs. She would wait until they were both healed enough to complete the mating. Now that she knew it *would* happen, she could breathe for the first time in what felt like forever.

"Welcome to the Pack," Kade said softly. "And when you're mated, we'll do it more officially. Thank you for saving my son. And as for those who would hurt you? We will find out who was working with those two humans. Of that, have no doubt."

He hugged his son, Melanie following suit, and then they left Brynn and Finn alone in the exam room with North.

The doctor smiled, his wolf in his eyes. "I need to check on you two. The other doctor, Noah, was outside in the waiting room with a lot of the Pack and Finn's family. He will make sure Hannah, Mark, and Walker will be okay. But let me check you two out and then you need to sleep. Mating and retribution will come. For now, just thank the goddess you have each other."

She leaned into her mate, knowing what North said was true. Her mate was wolf through and through. The damage the demon had done was gone.

Finally.

And soon, she'd have her bond, her mate, and her future.

Everything.

ADVANTAGE

Charles McMaster stared at the two dead bodies on the slab showing on the screen in front of him and held in a curse. The wolves had been stronger than he'd thought. According to his research, no wolf should have been able to break though those bindings. They would have to make them stronger for next time.

Because, of course, there would be a next time. This was merely one move in an elaborate chess game. He would not fail. He never did.

"Burn the bodies and make sure the ashes are spread apart. Make this building disappear, as well." It wouldn't do to have any connections to this. As it was, he was on a secure call, but again, he couldn't be too careful.

"Of course, sir." The soldier did as he was told and ended the call.

Charles ran a hand over his face and frowned. He'd wanted to know more about the two wolves who were from different Packs but seemed to be in a relationship. Brynn and Finn had become the face of the wolves, and humans were starting to side with them. That wouldn't do.

He would have to use the violence against them to his advantage. After all, if it looked as if he were looking into the violent outbursts for the sake of their people, humans would begin to side with him. Only the humans didn't know they would be doing so until it was too late.

Sheep.

The lot of them.

He'd just make sure the humans didn't know the wolf in sheep's clothing wasn't a wolf at all.

He'd use anything he could to his advantage. And one day, the wolves would die and he would use their power for his own needs.

Advantage.

Perfection.

CHAPTER FIFTEEN

Finn was beyond ready. *Beyond* it. He rolled over on his back and threw his arm over his eyes. It had been four days since he'd died and come back stronger and more connected to his wolf. Charlotte had moved out of the house quietly, leaving him and Brynn to be together. He hadn't asked for that. In fact, he had planned to find a new home on his own. But Charlotte had been her normal self and smiled before slapping the back of his head, saying that she could do it quickly and find a new place, that he'd need time alone with Brynn. His cousin knew him better than most.

He was fully healed—as was the woman sleeping next to him. The fact that he was merely *sleeping* next to Brynn in his bed rather than completing the mating made him edgy as hell. It was funny, they'd made love before so this wouldn't be a new thing, and yet he was freaking nervous.

What if he wasn't truly fixed?

What if he could feel the potential bond, but couldn't complete the mating?

Of course, as soon as he thought that, he felt like an asshole. The past four days had not only been about healing, but finding who had kidnapped them. The two who had come at them were dead, but there were more. There would always be more.

Finn was beyond weary, as well.

"Stop thinking so hard," Brynn murmured from his side.

He rolled over and put his head in his hand so he could watch her wake up. She smiled at him, her eyelashes fluttering awake.

"Good morning, mate."

She licked her lips. "Good morning, mate."

He groaned as she reached between them, cupping him through his boxer briefs. They'd been sleeping next to one another in their underwear for four days. Some would call it temptation; Finn called it another kind of agony.

"Are you feeling better today?" he asked, his fingers trailing along her skin. He couldn't stop touching her. His wolf pushed at him, a new feeling that settled him more than he thought it would. Damn, he'd missed so much of his life by not being able to hear his wolf fully. He knew going in that he'd take in every aspect of this newfound connection to his wolf and the woman in front of him and never take them for granted.

"Yes," she whispered, her hand squeezing his cock.

He let out a moan, rocking himself into her palm. "Brynn..."

"Don't Brynn me. It's time, Finn. Make love to me. Fuck me. Do it all. Just be *inside* me. I want the bond. You want it, too." There wasn't an uncertainty to her voice. His dominant mate knew what she wanted, and damn if she wasn't going to get it.

He fucking loved her.

He lowered his lips, kissing her softly. "Of course, I want our bond. I just wanted to make sure you were ready." He cupped her face, his thumb running along her cheekbone. "I didn't want to hurt you. I'll *never* hurt you, princess."

Brynn turned her head and sucked his thumb into her mouth. He groaned at the sight. "I know you won't. I'm healed, and so are you. So let's stop waiting and do what we should have been able to do so long ago."

Finn opened his mouth to say something, but then he could only moan. Loudly. Brynn scooted down and pulled his cock out of his boxers. When her tongue slid along the slit, he about came right then. Talk about embarrassing.

She swallowed the tip, her eyes on his as she teased him.

"Brynn. Fuck. Your mouth." He used to be better at the use of the English language.

She pulled back, a cocky grin on her face. "I'm going to taste all of you, Finn. And yeah, you can fuck my mouth. That's why I'm down here." She went back to what she was doing, rolling his balls in her hand while bobbing her head up and down. With each stroke, each lick, she went deeper, encasing him in such a wet heat that he had to hold back from coming.

"I love your mouth," he whispered then pulled her up by her shoulders. "But I need to be inside you. Now." He kissed her and ripped the side of her panties with his claw, leaving her bare. "Ride me."

She rolled her eyes and slid her leg over him, slowly, oh so slowly, lowering her body over his cock.

"Sweet goddess," she groaned. "Was it this good before?" She rolled her hips, causing Finn's eyes to cross. She pulled up her tank, leaving her breasts bare. Damn he loved her nipples.

He reached up and cupped her breasts, rolling her nipples between his fingers. "We've always been better than good, Brynn. But now? It's so much more." He lifted up, meeting her stroke for stroke. Her cunt squeezed him hard, and he almost came, but not without her. Never without her.

He slid his hands up and down her body, craving the feel of her skin beneath his palms. He loved this woman, this warrior, this wolf. She was everything and more. He'd dreamt of finding a mate, but it had never been to the true depth of Brynn. She was so much more than a dream, so much more than an ideal mate. She was real, unapologetic, and *his*. But it wasn't that he owned her, far from it. No, he was hers as much as the opposite. They were each other's, their respective fated mates, and yet fate was only a small part of it. He'd craved her without knowing that fate wanted him to. He'd begged for a change with her and he'd gotten his promise, his dream. She was his everything, and he would live the rest of his life showing her that he was worth it.

"Mark me," he groaned. "Mark me and make me yours."

She threw her head back and rode him with abandon before falling on his chest. He tilted his head to the side and fell onto the edge of bliss as she bit into him, marking him forever. A part of him he hadn't known existed locked into place, a tug on the new thread of connection and fate strengthening.

"Your turn." She moved to the side, baring her shoulder and neck for him.

His wolf howled, begging for more. He let his fangs slide out of his gums and bit into her shoulder, marking her. The thread between them pulsated then locked into another seal of promise and forever.

He slid his fangs out then rolled them over, pounding into her as she lifted her hips, meeting him thrust for thrust.

"Come with me, Brynn, my mate." He crushed his mouth to hers, kissing her with all of his heart, his soul.

And when her cunt clamped around him, her body bowing, he followed, filling her until they were both spent, sweaty, and sated. The final part of the mating bond, the part that connected the two humans as well as the wolves slid into place, and he warmed.

"I can feel you," she whimpered, awe in her voice.

Tears slid down her cheeks, and Finn kissed them away one by one. "I can feel you, too." And he did. A warm strength that would hold him up if he should fall. Some mates, over time, felt deeper connections and even had powers along the bond. One day, they might, too. But for now, he had her and her wolf. He didn't need anything else.

Brynn's eyes widened and she opened her mouth on a scream.

Finn rolled, sitting them both up even as he kept deep within her. "What's wrong?"

She put her hand above her heart and gave him a sheepish smile. "I wasn't prepared for the other part."

He frowned and ran his hands up and down her arms. "What part? Are you okay? What's wrong?"

"I'm a Redwood now," she murmured. "When I mated with you, the bonds brought me over to this Pack. I screamed because I had to sever my connection to the Talons first. I've never *not* felt my brothers. It was...weird."

He kissed her cheeks, her lips. "I'm sorry, Brynn. I know it's hard." He swallowed. "If it were possible, I'd have moved over to the Talons."

She cupped his face. "I know. And I'm not sad that I'm a Redwood. It's just different. You're the Heir, and now I'm your mate. It was always going to be this way. Kade accepted me into the Pack, and that's why it happened so fast. If I hadn't been willing, then it would have been different. So just kiss me, mate, and celebrate with me. I won't mourn what I've lost because I've gained so much."

He kissed her as she'd asked, bringing her chest to his so he could feel her heartbeat along his skin and the bond.

"I love you."

"I love you, too." She smiled at him, her eyes sparkling. "Now, how about we test that shifter endurance."

He snorted then rolled her under him, the movement pulling a groan out of both of them. "Sounds like a plan."

He'd gladly do this every day until the end of time. He had his mate, his Brynn. He didn't need anything else.

"If you don't stop smiling like that, I'm going to punch you," Brynn said from his side.

Finn smiled a bit wider and brought their clasped hands up to his mouth. "I love you, and I'm walking to the café where I fell in love with you. You're my mate, and I can feel your wolf. I can't stop smiling."

She rolled her eyes but smiled, as well. "You're ruining your big bad wolf reputation."

"Gladly. For you."

"Dork."

"Your dork."

"Goddess. If I had known you'd be this mushy..."

"What? You'd just mate me again?" He stole a kiss and kept walking. She leaned into him, and he smiled again. Fuck. He needed to stop smiling so hard. But he couldn't help it. They'd spent the rest of the day yesterday in bed until they both could barely walk and were in dire need of food and water. Seriously, the best way to spend a day.

Now, they were back to what they had been doing before—proving to the world that wolves were people, too. It shouldn't matter to the humans that shifters were stronger, faster, and could kill. Humans, as they'd proven, could kill, as well. Humans were a threat just as much as shifters. It depended on the individual if the threat was carried out.

The Packs still didn't know who'd kidnapped them beyond the two they had met face to face. They did not know who was in charge. That, above all else, scared him. Because they couldn't continue to fight an enemy they did not know. But they did know the two men who'd attacked them were not alone. There had to be a connection to someone else, and Finn knew the Redwoods and Talons would find it. They had protected their Packs for centuries before this. They had defeated a demon from the very depths of hell. They would find a way to defend themselves from humans.

Humans.

Those without magic or the ability to shift. Yet their greatest enemy.

His Pack's pain, the Talons' pain, Franklin's *death,* would not be in vain.

Brynn squeezed Finn's hand, and he looked down at her, only to have the hair on the back of his neck stand on end. A group of seven humans came toward them, their hands fisted at their sides and glares on their faces.

Shit.

He was not in the fucking mood to deal with this. He was just walking outside on a sidewalk with his mate. He hadn't shifted, he wasn't even growling or letting his wolf come to the surface. If it hadn't been him and Brynn, whose faces were clear to the public as known shifters, no one would have recognized their true natures.

Sadly, he had a feeling he was about to see the true natures of those in front of him.

And he wasn't going to like it.

"You should just go back to your dens. We don't need your kind here."

Brynn tilted her head as the man spoke. Finn held on to her hand. Their Alpha had told them that this would be their last outing like this. Things had changed. They were to show they were alive and well to those who may be watching, but after that, the world would have to know that though they might look harmless, and would be to anyone who didn't harm them, they would never be defenseless.

It had come to this, though it was inevitable.

The world was scared of the unknown, and those in command weren't ready to show their true motives. The next step was coming, and Finn was ready to defend those he considered his when it happened.

Because he knew there was no way they were coming out of this unscathed. No, not today, not with these people in front of him. But over the long haul. As soon as the Packs took down one cell, one group, or a pair of people, another would pop up into place. They were scattered, their forces unsure and fighting on too many fronts. There would come a time where they would have to band together, and Finn wasn't sure those he loved would come out of it whole.

And damn it, that was not what he wanted.

He wanted peace.

Only, he knew he'd have to fight for it.

"We are going to go get coffee, and you will be leaving us alone," Finn said, his voice calm. Too calm—though the humans didn't know it.

"I said you should go," the human male repeated.

"We aren't doing anything wrong," Brynn said, her voice sharp. "You're in our way. We will call the authorities if we have to."

Finn ran a tongue over his teeth. They knew some people on the local police force, but he wasn't sure whose side those who showed up would be on. His allegiance was to Pack first, all others second. And now it seemed he might have to show that in a more public fashion.

"You're a threat to our children," a softer-spoken man said. "If you'd just stay away like you were, everything would be fine."

Finn shook his head. "We aren't a threat to your children. If anything, the actions of those who hate us are a threat to *our* children. The thing is, you say that we should go back to when we were hidden? But we weren't truly hidden before. We walked amongst you, and were friends with you and your neighbors. We held jobs, and married those we loved. We had children. We grew up with one another, and yet now you've all seemed to forget that."

Brynn continued for him. "Before you learned to fear us, we were one of you. Now that you think you know who we are, you listen to the lies told about us rather than what you see about us, and you think we should hide away. Or worse, you try to kill us." She waved her hand at them. "Look at you. Seven against two, and yet all we have done is walk down a sidewalk holding hands. How is that okay? How is that normal?"

"You aren't normal," one of them said.

"No. I guess we aren't," Finn agreed. "But then again, are you? Are any of us normal? We aren't human. I will give you that. But we haven't hurt you. We want to be able to live in peace. But it's hard when just this week, someone kidnapped the woman I love as well as myself, cut into us with knives, and beat us. How is that okay?"

"And where are these people?"

"How are you healed now?"

Finn let out a curse. These people wouldn't understand. They wouldn't until something happened to make them understand. Only Finn didn't know what that was. He'd damn well figure it out in the near future, though. They all had to.

"We will not stand for you hurting our children, our families," Finn said, his voice firm. You lived with us once, and I hope that one day you will do so again." He faced one onlooker who held a phone, the camera facing him. "We are not the animals you fear, but if you hurt our children, if you bomb us and threaten to kill us, then we will show you the strength we have. We are wolves, but we are not evil."

With that, he turned his back to the humans. Brynn following suit. They'd tried acting as if they weren't a threat and they'd been hurt. His *mate* had been hurt. It was time the humans knew the truth behind what they feared. The shifters wouldn't hurt those who didn't hurt them, but maybe it was good that some feared them.

Shifters were dominant predators for a reason.

He and Brynn made it back to his car and then drove back to the den in silence. Brynn hadn't fully moved in yet, but she had most of her stuff at his place. Thinking of little things like that helped him keep his wolf in check. As it was, he wanted to shift and roam through the forest, in need of nature and their connections.

"Well, Kade told us to show our strength," Brynn said wryly. "I guess words are a form of strength today. I'm glad we didn't have to show that strength another way."

He gripped her hand as he made his way through the den wards and toward their home. "I hate that we left and didn't make it to the café, but I wasn't in the mood to fight them. They might have had weapons. But worse, we would have had to show the humans exactly how strong we are physically. And I wasn't in the mood for them to catch that on camera."

"Again," Brynn said softly. "They've seen us fighting before, and they will again."

"It's not over."

"Nope. And I fear it won't be for a while."

When they pulled up to his—not *their*—home, he turned off the car then pulled her hand to his, brushing his lips over her skin.

She leaned over the console and kissed his shoulder. His wolf nudged at him, and he smiled, despite the climate of the world around him. He had his mate and his wolf, that had to count for something.

They got out of the car and went inside. He turned on the TV, needing background noise, and wanting to know if what had happened had made the local news. It was most likely on social media sites, and their team within the Pack that dealt with monitoring that would have reports for him and the Alpha soon.

"We are aware of the violence occurring between us and the ones that call themselves shifters."

Us.

That was a telling word.

"Brynn, come listen," Finn said as he watched Senator McMaster talk to the camera, a wooden podium in front of him, and an American flag behind him.

"Dear, goddess," Brynn murmured. "He's putting humans against wolves but on a national scale now."

"I'm texting Dad." His phone beeped. "They're already watching."

"We are looking into these people. We will not allow fear to overrule our actions and society. We will protect our own." McMaster faced the camera head on. "At all costs."

With that, he answered a few questions with non-answers, but it all left Finn with a cold feeling down his spine.

"He didn't declare war, but damn close," Brynn snapped. "And what about the President? Has he said anything? Damn it. We have wolves in Senate seats. Are they going to speak now?"

Finn ran a hand over his face and shook his head. "We knew it was coming. Those wolves in Senate seats will do what needs to be done. It's not about the Talons or the Redwoods. It's about all of us. All of our people. I don't know what is going to happen next, but we aren't helpless here."

"I know, but I still feel sick."

He held her close, his wolf nudging harder at him. "Me, too, Brynn. Me, too."

The next step in the Unveiling had begun, and Finn didn't know what would happen. They had tried to project the face of calm and peace, and he prayed that some of those who had watched had seen it and been convinced. He didn't want to think of the alternative.

The wolves were out, and those in power on the human side were coming.

It had begun.

LEAH

Leah ran behind her twin brother, her pulse racing in her throat. They were coming. They *knew*. Roland reached out behind him, and she pushed his hand away.

"Keep going. I can keep up. Don't worry about me and end up tripping."

She wished she could pull on the water around them to protect her and her brother, but it was too dangerous. With those behind him and her body wearing down after running for far too long, using magic would be a death sentence.

"I'm not leaving you behind, Leah. So run your fucking ass off. There's a safe house up the road." He grinned over his shoulder, that lock of hair she loved falling over his forehead. "I'll never lead you astray, little sister."

She smiled at him despite the fact that they were both running for their lives. "You're not that much older than me, Ro."

"It's enough. Now let's go."

He turned back, only to freeze in his tracks. It took a minute for the crack in the air to register to her. Roland fell to his knees, and Leah screamed.

"Roland!"

She raised her hands, the water on the leaves of the trees from that morning's rainfall rising into the air with her pain, her agony.

Another crack in the air.

A gunshot. That's what that was.

A sizzling pain along her side, a fiery heat that wouldn't be quenched by the water at her fingertips. She tried to breathe, only to cough, her legs going out from under her.

She fell beside her brother, her arms reaching for him, only to come up short.

Roland lay at an odd angle, his face toward her. His eyes wide, unseeing in death. While the shot had hit her in the side, his had hit him directly in the chest.

Her brother, her twin, her fellow witch.

Gone.

The darkness came, and she didn't fight. She'd been running for so long, and now she had nothing left.

Only hollowness.

They had come for the witches...and they had won.

EPILOGUE

Brynn held back a groan as she finished shifting back to human. It had been her first hunt with the Redwoods, and it had gone well. Now she and Finn were safely behind the den wards and she *really* wanted to jump him. Of course, she always wanted to jump him so this wasn't really different than most days.

They hadn't been outside the wards in the past three days. Not since the broadcast from McMaster. They would eventually, but right now, they were regrouping and ensuring their Pack was whole and healthy before anything else came at them.

She was using this time to get used to the idea of a new Pack. She missed her Talons like crazy, but with the underground tunnels and phones, she spoke with and saw them almost daily.

She would be fine. And she'd be a fucking amazing Redwood.

"I love the sight of your naked ass in the moonlight," Finn drawled.

Brynn rolled her eyes. "Thanks." She wiggled for him, and he groaned.

She turned for him and almost swallowed her tongue at the sight of him naked, hard, and *hers*.

"Damn, you're fucking gorgeous." She didn't realize she'd said that aloud until Finn winked at her.

"Thank you, darling." He moved closer. "What do you say we—"

A gunshot.

The scent of blood.

A scream.

Another gunshot.

More blood.

"Finn."

He ran toward the sound and she cursed, following him. They were far away from the others now because she'd wanted time alone with him. She hoped others would come, as she didn't have a phone on her. But damn it, if a Pack member were hurt, this would mean war for sure.

"Damn it. It's right outside the wards." Finn growled and kept moving, *through* the wards.

She followed. It didn't matter that it might be a trap. Someone was hurt, and they weren't going to let someone die because they were afraid. That wasn't who they were. That wasn't who wolves were.

They made their way to a small clearing, their claws out, and on high alert. On the dirt ahead of them were two bodies, a male and a female. Both lay in pools of blood. Brynn inhaled deeply and cursed.

"Witches. Finn, they're both witches. I don't scent anyone else. Whoever did this is long gone."

Finn knelt naked beside both of them. "He's gone, but she has a weak pulse. Fuck. I don't recognize them as part of the covens we work with, but we can't leave them here."

Brynn knelt down as well, as Finn worked to help the woman. She checked both bodies for weapons and didn't find any. "Are we bringing them to the den?"

Finn nodded. "We have to. She'll die without medical care. And damn it, if they were running this way, they might have been running towards us for help. I don't know, but we don't have long."

She nodded and lifted the man over her shoulder in a fireman's carry. "Take her and run. I'll be behind you. You're faster than me."

He picked the woman up, careful of her wounds. "Be *right* behind me. Just because we can't scent others, doesn't mean they aren't there. Not anymore."

"I know," Brynn said fiercely. "Now go, mate of mine. I love you. Don't be stupid and get hurt."

"Love you, too, Brynn darling."

With that, he turned and ran, the dying woman in his arms. Brynn followed, her pace just as brutal. Someone had killed and injured witches near Redwood and Talon land. That couldn't be a coincidence.

Not anymore.

The world was at a tipping point. One wrong move, and it would all crumble around them. She only prayed that she'd be able to hold on in the aftermath. Because now she had her mate, her one true path. She'd found her Finn, her soul. And no matter what, she wouldn't let him out of her grasp.

Fate had given her a choice and she'd taken it.

Now it was up to the world to make theirs.

THE END

Next in the Talon Pack World....
Ryder finds the path he's been missing.

A Note from Carrie Ann

Thank you so much for reading **AN ALPHA'S CHOICE**. I do hope if you liked this story, that you would please leave a review. Not only does a review spread the word to other readers, they let us authors know if you'd like to see more stories like this from us. I love hearing from readers and talking to them when I can. If you want to make sure you know what's coming next from me, you can sign up for my newsletter at www.CarrieAnnRyan.com; follow me on twitter at @CarrieAnnRyan, or like my Facebook page. I also have a Facebook Fan Club where we have trivia, chats, and other goodies. You guys are the reason I get to do what I do and I thank you.

Make sure you're signed up for my MAILING LIST so you can know when the next releases are available as well as find giveaways and FREE READS.

The Talon Pack series is an ongoing series. I hope you get a chance to catch up!

The Talon Pack (Following the Redwood Pack Series):
Book 1: Tattered Loyalties
Book 2: An Alpha's Choice
Book 3: Mated in Mist (Coming in 2016)

About Carrie Ann and her Books

New York Times and USA Today Bestselling Author Carrie Ann Ryan never thought she'd be a writer. Not really. No, she loved math and science and even went on to graduate school in chemistry. Yes, she read as a kid and devoured teen fiction and Harry Potter, but it wasn't until someone handed her a romance book in her late teens that she realized that there was something out there just for her. When another author suggested she use the voices in her head for good and not evil, The Redwood Pack and all her other stories were born.

Carrie Ann is a bestselling author of over twenty novels and novellas and has so much more on her mind (and on her spreadsheets *grins*) that she isn't planning on giving up her dream anytime soon.

www.CarrieAnnRyan.com

Redwood Pack Series:
Book 1: An Alpha's Path
Book 2: A Taste for a Mate
Book 3: Trinity Bound
Book 3.5: A Night Away
Book 4: Enforcer's Redemption
Book 4.5: Blurred Expectations
Book 4.7: Forgiveness
Book 5: Shattered Emotions
Book 6: Hidden Destiny
Book 6.5: A Beta's Haven
Book 7: Fighting Fate
Book 7.5 Loving the Omega

Book 7.7: The Hunted Heart
Book 8: Wicked Wolf

The Talon Pack (Following the Redwood Pack Series):
Book 1: Tattered Loyalties
Book 2: An Alpha's Choice
Book 3: Mated in Mist (Coming in 2016)

The Redwood Pack Volumes:
Redwood Pack Vol 1
Redwood Pack Vol 2
Redwood Pack Vol 3
Redwood Pack Vol 4
Redwood Pack Vol 5
Redwood Pack Vol 6

Montgomery Ink:
Book 0.5: Ink Inspired
Book 0.6: Ink Reunited
Book 1: Delicate Ink
Book 1.5 Forever Ink
Book 2: Tempting Boundaries
Book 3: Harder than Words
Book 4: Written in Ink (Coming Oct 2015)

The Branded Pack Series:
(Written with Alexandra Ivy)
Books 1 & 2: Stolen and Forgiven
Books 3 & 4: Abandoned and Unseen (Coming Sept 2015)

Dante's Circle Series:
Book 1: Dust of My Wings
Book 2: Her Warriors' Three Wishes
Book 3: An Unlucky Moon
The Dante's Circle Box Set (Contains Books 1-3)

Book 3.5: His Choice
Book 4: Tangled Innocence
Book 5: Fierce Enchantment
Book 6: An Immortal's Song (Coming in 2016)

Holiday, Montana Series:
Book 1: Charmed Spirits
Book 2: Santa's Executive
Book 3: Finding Abigail
The Holiday Montana Box Set (Contains Books 1-3)
Book 4: Her Lucky Love
Book 5: Dreams of Ivory

Excerpt: Wicked Wolf

**From New York Times Bestselling Author
Carrie Ann Ryan's Redwood Pack Series**

There were times to drool over a sexy wolf.

Sitting in the middle of a war room disguised as a
board meeting was not one of those times.

Gina Jamenson did her best not to stare at the
dark-haired, dark-eyed man across the room. The hint
of ink peeking out from under his shirt made her want
to pant. She *loved* ink and this wolf clearly had a lot of
it. Her own wolf within nudged at her, a soft brush
beneath her skin, but she ignored her. When her wolf
whimpered, Gina promised herself that she'd go on a
long run in the forest later. She didn't understand why
her wolf was acting like this, but she'd deal with it
when she was in a better place. She just couldn't let
her wolf have control right then—even for a man such
as the gorgeous specimen a mere ten feet from her.

Today was more important than the wants and
feelings of a half wolf, half witch hybrid.

Today was the start of a new beginning.

At least that's what her dad had told her.

Considering her father was also the Alpha of the
Redwood Pack, he would be in the know. She'd been
adopted into the family when she'd been a young girl.
A rogue wolf during the war had killed her parents,
setting off a long line of events that had changed her
life.

As it was, Gina wasn't quite sure how she'd ended
up in the meeting between the two Packs, the
Redwoods and the Talons. Sure, the Packs had met

before over the past fifteen years of their treaty, but this meeting seemed different.

This one seemed more important somehow.

And they'd invited—more like *demanded*—Gina to attend.

At twenty-six, she knew she was the youngest wolf in the room by far. Most of the wolves were around her father's age, somewhere in the hundreds. The dark-eyed wolf might have been slightly younger than that, but only slightly if the power radiating off of him was any indication.

Wolves lived a long, long time. She'd heard stories of her people living into their thousands, but she'd never met any of the wolves who had. The oldest wolf she'd met was a friend of the family, Emeline, who was over five hundred. That number boggled her mind even though she'd grown up knowing the things that went bump in the night were real.

Actually, she *was* one of the things that went bump in the night.

"Are we ready to begin?" Gideon, the Talon Alpha, asked, his voice low. It held that dangerous edge that spoke of power and authority.

Her wolf didn't react the way most wolves would, head and eyes down, shoulders dropped. Maybe if she'd been a weaker wolf, she'd have bowed to his power, but as it was, her wolf was firmly entrenched within the Redwoods. Plus, it wasn't as if Gideon was *trying* to make her bow just then. No, those words had simply been spoken in his own voice.

Commanding without even trying.

Then again, he *was* an Alpha.

Kade, her father, looked around the room at each of his wolves and nodded. "Yes. It is time."

Their formality intrigued her. Yes, they were two Alphas who held a treaty and worked together in times of war, but she had thought they were also friends.

Maybe today was even more important than she'd realized.

Gideon released a sigh that spoke of years of angst and worries. She didn't know the history of the Talons as well as she probably should have, so she didn't know exactly why there was always an air of sadness and pain around the Alpha.

Maybe after this meeting, she'd be able to find out more.

Of course, in doing so, she'd have to *not* look at a certain wolf in the corner. His gaze was so intense she was sure he was studying her. She felt it down in her bones, like a fiery caress that promised something more.

Or maybe she was just going crazy and needed to find a wolf to scratch the itch.

She might not be looking for a mate, but she wouldn't say no to something else. Wolves were tactile creatures after all.

"Gina?"

She blinked at the sound of Kade's voice and turned to him.

She was the only one standing other than the two wolves in charge of security—her uncle Adam, the Enforcer, and the dark-eyed wolf.

Well, *that* was embarrassing.

She kept her head down and forced herself not to blush. From the heat on her neck, she was pretty sure she'd failed in the latter.

"Sorry," she mumbled then sat down next to another uncle, Jasper, the Beta of the Pack.

Although the Alphas had called this meeting, she wasn't sure what it would entail. Each Alpha had come with their Beta, a wolf in charge of security...and her father had decided to bring her.

Her being there didn't make much sense in the grand scheme of things since it put the power on the Redwoods' side, but she wasn't about to question authority in front of another Pack. That at least had been ingrained in her training.

"Let's get started then," Kade said after he gave her a nod. "Gideon? Do you want to begin?"

Gina held back a frown. They *were* acting more formal than usual, so that hadn't been her imagination. The Talons and the Redwoods had formed a treaty during the latter days of the war between the Redwoods and the Centrals. It wasn't as though these were two newly acquainted Alphas meeting for the first time. Though maybe when it came to Pack matters, Alphas couldn't truly be friends.

What a lonely way to live.

"It's been fifteen years since the end of the Central War, yet there hasn't been a single mating between the two Packs," Gideon said, shocking her.

Gina blinked. Really? That couldn't be right. She was sure there had to have been *some* cross-Pack mating.

Right?

"That means that regardless of the treaties we signed, we don't believe the moon goddess has seen fit to fully accept us as a unit," Kade put in.

"What do you mean?" she asked, then shut her mouth. She was the youngest wolf here and wasn't formally titled or ranked. She should *not* be speaking right now.

She felt the gaze of the dark-eyed wolf on her, but she didn't turn to look. Instead, she kept her head down in a show of respect to the Alphas.

"You can ask questions, Gina. It's okay," Kade said, the tone of his voice not changing, but, as his daughter, she heard the softer edge. "And what I mean is, mating comes from the moon goddess. Yes, we can find our own versions of mates by not bonding fully, but a true bond, a true potential mate, is chosen by the moon goddess. That's how it's always been in the past."

Gideon nodded. "There haven't been many matings within the Talons in general."

Gina sucked in a breath, and the Beta of the Talons, Mitchell, turned her way. "Yes," Mitchell said softly. "It's that bad. It could be that in this period of change within our own pack hierarchy, our members just haven't found mates yet, but that doesn't seem likely. There's something else going on."

Gina knew Gideon—as well as the rest of his brothers and cousins—had come into power at some point throughout the end of the Central War during a period of the Talon's own unrest, but she didn't know the full history. She wasn't even sure Kade or the rest of the Pack royalty did.

There were some things that were intensely private within a Pack that could not—and should not—be shared.

Jasper tapped his fingers along the table. As the Redwood Beta, it was his job to care for their needs and recognize hidden threats that the Enforcer and Alpha might not see. The fact that he was here told Gina that the Pack could be in trouble from something *within* the Pack, rather than an outside force that Adam, the Enforcer, would be able to see through his own bonds and power.

"Since Finn became the Heir to the Pack at such a young age, it has changed a few things on our side," Jasper said softly. Finn was her brother, Melanie and

Kade's oldest biological child. "The younger generation will be gaining their powers and bonds to the goddess earlier than would otherwise be expected." Her uncle looked at her, and she kept silent. "That means the current Pack leaders will one day not have the bonds we have to our Pack now. But like most healthy Packs, that doesn't mean we're set aside. It only means we will be there to aid the new hierarchy while they learn their powers. That's how it's always been in our Pack, and in others, but it's been a very long time since it's happened to us."

"Gina will one day be the Enforcer," Adam said from behind her. "I don't know when, but it will be soon. The other kids aren't old enough yet to tell who will take on which role, but since Gina is in her twenties, the shifts are happening."

The room grew silent, with an odd sense of change settling over her skin like an electric blanket turned on too high.

She didn't speak. She'd known about her path, had dreamed the dreams from the moon goddess herself. But that didn't mean she wanted the Talons to know all of this. It seemed...private somehow.

"What does this have to do with mating?" she asked, wanting to focus on something else.

Gideon gave her a look, and she lowered her eyes. He might not be her Alpha, but he was still a dominant wolf. Yes, she hadn't lowered her eyes before, but she'd been rocked a bit since Adam had told the others of her future. She didn't want to antagonize anyone when Gideon clearly wanted to show his power. Previously, everything had been casual; now it clearly was not.

Kade growled beside her. "Gideon."

The Talon Alpha snorted, not smiling, but moved his gaze. "It's fun to see how she reacts."

"She's my daughter and the future Enforcer."

"*She* is right here, so how about you answer my question?"

Jasper chuckled by her side, and Gina wondered how quickly she could reach the nearest window and jump. It couldn't be that far. She wouldn't die from the fall or anything, and she'd be able to run home.

Quickly.

"Mating," Kade put in, the laughter in his eyes fading, "is only a small part of the problem. When we sent Caym back to hell with the other demons, it changed the power structure within the Packs as well as outside them. The Centrals who fought against us died because they'd lost their souls to the demon. The Centrals that had hidden from the old Alphas ended up being lone wolves. They're not truly a Pack yet because the goddess hasn't made anyone an Alpha."

"Then you have the Redwoods, with a hierarchy shift within the younger generation," Gideon said. "And the Talons' new power dynamic is only fifteen years old, and we haven't had a mating in long enough that it's starting to worry us."

"Not that you'd say that to the rest of the Pack," Mitchell mumbled.

"It's best they don't know," Gideon said, the sounds of an old argument telling Gina there was more going on here than what they revealed.

Interesting.

"There aren't any matings between our two Packs, and I know the trust isn't fully there," Kade put in then sighed. "I don't know how to fix that myself. I don't think I can."

"You're the Alpha," Jasper said calmly. "If you *tell* them to get along with the other wolves, they will, and for the most part, they have. But it isn't as authentic as if they find that trust on their own. We've let them go this long on their own, but now, I think we need to find another way to have our Packs more entwined."

The dark-eyed wolf came forward then. "You've seen something," he growled.

Dear goddess. His voice.

Her wolf perked, and she shoved her down. This wasn't the time.

"We've seen...something, Quinn," Kade answered.

Quinn. That was his name.

Sexy.

And again, *so* not the time.

Find out more in Wicked Wolf. Out Now.

Tattered Loyalties

**From New York Times Bestselling Author
Carrie Ann Ryan's Talon Pack Series**

When the great war between the Redwoods and
the Centrals occurred three decades ago, the Talon
Pack risked their lives for the side of good. After
tragedy struck, Gideon Brentwood became the Alpha
of the Talons. But the Pack's stability is threatened,
and he's forced to take mate—only the one fate puts in
his path is the woman he shouldn't want.

Though the daughter of the Redwood Pack's Beta,
Brie Jamenson has known peace for most of her life.
When she finds the man who could be her mate, she's
shocked to discover Gideon is the Alpha wolf of the
Talon Pack. As a submissive, her strength lies in her
heart, not her claws. But if her new Pack disagrees or
disapproves, the consequences could be fatal.

As the worlds Brie and Gideon have always known
begin to shift, they must face their challenges together
in order to help their Pack and seal their bond. But
when the Pack is threatened from the inside, Gideon
doesn't know who he can trust and Brie's life could be
forfeit in the crossfire. It will take the strength of an
Alpha and the courage of his mate to realize where
true loyalties lie.

Find out more in Tattered Loyalties. Out Now.

Delicate Ink

**From New York Times Bestselling Author
Carrie Ann Ryan's Montgomery Ink Series**

On the wrong side of thirty, Austin Montgomery is
ready to settle down. Unfortunately, his inked sleeves
and scruffy beard isn't the suave business appearance
some women crave. Only finding a woman who can
deal with his job, as a tattoo artist and owner of
Montgomery Ink, his seven meddling siblings, and his
own gruff attitude won't be easy.

Finding a man is the last thing on Sierra Elder's
mind. A recent transplant to Denver, her focus is on
opening her own boutique. Wanting to cover up scars
that run deeper than her flesh, she finds in Austin a
man that truly gets to her—in more ways than one.

Although wary, they embark on a slow,
tempestuous burn of a relationship. When blasts from
both their pasts intrude on their present, however, it
will take more than a promise of what could be to
keep them together.

Find out more in Delicate Ink. Out Now.

Dust of My Wings

**From New York Times Bestselling Author
Carrie Ann Ryan's Dante's Circle Series**

*Humans aren't as alone as they choose to believe.
Every human possesses a trait of supernatural that
lays dormant within their genetic make-up.
Centuries of diluting and breeding have allowed
humans to think they are alone and untouched by
magic. But what happens when something changes?*

Neat freak lab tech, Lily Banner lives her life as
any ordinary human. She's dedicated to her work and
loves to hang out with her friends at Dante's Circle,
their local bar. When she discovers a strange blue dust
at work she meets a handsome stranger holding
secrets – and maybe her heart. But after a close call
with a thunderstorm, she may not be as ordinary as
she thinks.

Shade Griffin is a warrior angel sent to Earth to
protect the supernaturals' secrets. One problem, he
can't stop leaving dust in odd places around town.
Now he has to find every ounce of his dust and keep
the presence of the supernatural a secret. But after a
close encounter with a sexy lab tech and a lightning
quick connection, his millennia old loyalties may shift
and he could lose more than just his wings in the
chaos.

Warning: Contains a sexy angel with a choice to
make and a green-eyed lab tech who dreams of a dark-
winged stranger. Oh yeah, and a shocking spark that's
sure to leave them begging for more.

Find out more in Dust of My Wings. Out Now.

Made in the USA
San Bernardino, CA
03 June 2017